A World
in Our Hands

*Written, Illustrated, and Edited
by Young People of the World*

IN HONOR OF THE FIFTIETH ANNIVERSARY
OF THE UNITED NATIONS

**TRICYCLE PRESS
BERKELEY, CALIFORNIA**

**PEACE CHILD
INTERNATIONAL**

**PAINTBRUSH
DIPLOMACY**

■

Ō̊

TRICYCLE PRESS
P.O. Box 7123 • Berkeley, California 94707 • U.S.A.
Book Design: Siân Keogh, Axis Design, London
Cover Design: Siân Keogh, Catherine Jacobes, Nicole Geiger
Cover Illustration: Busaba Saw-Mag, Thailand
Produced by: Peace Child International
The White House, Buntingford, England SG9 9AH
in association with
Paintbrush Diplomacy
World Trade Center, Suite 103, San Francisco, California 94111 U.S.A.
All artwork in this book remains in the collections of these two nonprofit organizations.

For Peace Child
Project Director: David Woollcombe / **Assistant:** Rosey Simonds
Designers: José Luis Bayer & Ivonne Lacombe, Chile
Senior Editors: Danijela Zunec, 21, Croatia; Ulrich Gerza, 21, Austria;
Cecilia Weckström, 19, Finland; Alejandra Silvani, 20, Argentina
Editors: Eddy Abraham, 15, India; Andreanna Benitez, 12, Philippines; Mia Björkqvist, 20, Finland;
Susagna Boldu, 17, Spain; Maria Soledad Bumbacher, 20, Argentina; Illa Carilla, 16, Columbia;
Sarah Impens, 17, Belgium; Adriana Koe, 18, Australia; Magda Latosinska, 15, Poland; Omari Mtiga, 16, Tanzania;
Jordan Melic, 13, Singapore; Anuragini Nagar, 20, India; Jenny Pattinson, 16, United Kingdom; Shay Porat, 25, Israel;
Fahrekbussa Raad, 14, Jordan; Edwin Riley, 21, U.S.A.; Petrit Selimi, 15, Yugoslavia; Alejandra Silvani, 20, Argentina;
Anita Stefin, 17, Slovenia; Chihiro Tanaka, 17, Japan; Kansai Uchida, 12, U.S.A.; Vajda Vaitucte, 19, Lithuania;
Farida Vandendriessche, 18, Belgium; Portia Villanueva, 12, Philippines; Cassandra Watkins, 17, U.S.A.

For Paintbrush Diplomacy
Director: Germaine Juneau / **Director of School Programs:** Julie Wolfe

Thank you to Sean Keogh, Phyllis Richardson, Irene Baillie, and Jon Fedyk for their much appreciated expertise.

Permission to reprint the photograph of the Fresques de José Maria Sert on page 15
generously granted by the United Nations Office at Geneva.
The paintings on the cover and on pages 61 and 72–73 are supplied courtesy of
the Lions Club International and are used by permission.
The paintings on pages 47 (bottom right), 54, 64, 67, 88–89 are supplied courtesy of the
United Nations Fund for Population and are used by permission.
Permission to use the painting *Los Pucacungas* on pages 76–77, generously
granted by the Usko-Ayar Amazonian School of Painting ©.
Postage stamps reproduced on page 66 by permission of the United Nations Postal Administration.
**With thanks for the generous support from the Fundación Amalia Lacroze de Fortabat and the Foundation for
the Fiftieth Anniversary of the United Nations, Inc.**
Previous page: *José Luis Bayer, 28, Chile*

The opinions expressed in this book are those of the young authors, and not of the associated organizations.

Library of Congress Cataloging-in-Publication Data
A world in our hands : in honor of the 50th Anniversary of the United Nations : young people of the world.
p. cm. Includes index. Summary: A collaborative effort of the UN and children from 115 countries that includes poems, prose, and paintings
addressing the international organization's structure and youth involvement. ISBN 1-883672-31-7
1. United Nations—Anniversaries, etc.—Juvenile literature. [1. United Nations.] JX1977.W59 1995 341.23—dc20 95–16236 CIP AC

First Tricycle Press printing 1995
Manufactured in Hong Kong through Mandarin Offset

1 2 3 4 5 6 - 00 99 98 97 96 95

▲

Contents

Above: *Vajda Vatucte, 19, Lithuania*

Foreword

Fifty years ago, the nations of the world laid down their weapons, bringing an end to one of the most brutal conflicts in history. Determined to preserve that peace, and to secure a better future for all peoples, delegates from fifty states raised their pens in San Francisco to sign the Charter of the United Nations. The world organization was born.

Today, young people from across the globe have joined together to write a history of the United Nations in celebration of its fiftieth birthday. But their book, this book, is a gift to the world. Through their painting, prose and poetry, they share with us what the United Nations has meant to their communities, their countries, and the world over the past half-century. And with creativity and candor, they offer us a vision for progress into the next fifty years.

To young people everywhere this book sends a message: how the United Nations performs is your concern. Where the United Nations goes is your decision. So let the world know your fears and frustrations, your wishes, hopes and dreams. Only with your help can we ready the United Nations to serve the world of the future. Your future.

BOUTROS BOUTROS-GHALI
Secretary-General of the United Nations

Left: *Chihiro Tanaka, 17, Japan*

Charter *of the* United Nations

— Preamble —

WE THE PEOPLES OF THE UNITED NATIONS DETERMINED

to save succeeding generations from the scourge of war, which twice in our lifetime has brought untold sorrow to mankind, and to reaffirm faith in fundamental human rights, in the dignity and worth of the human person, in the equal rights of men and women and of nations large and small, and to establish conditions under which justice and respect for the obligations arising from treaties and other sources of international law can be maintained, and to promote social progress and better standards of life in larger freedom,

AND FOR THESE ENDS

to practice tolerance and live together in peace with one another as good neighbors, and to unite our strength to maintain international peace and security, and to ensure by the acceptance of principles and the institution of methods, that armed force shall not be used, save in the common interest, and to employ international machinery for the promotion of the economic and social advancement of all peoples,

HAVE RESOLVED TO COMBINE OUR EFFORTS
TO ACCOMPLISH THESE AIMS

Accordingly, our respective Governments, through representatives assembled in the city of San Francisco, who have exhibited their full powers found to be in good and due form, have agreed to the present Charter of the United Nations and do hereby establish an international organization to be known as the United Nations.

Signed at the United Nations Conference on International Organization on June 26th, 1945, San Francisco

Left: *Shreyashe Chakraborty, 8, India*

A *Charter of* **Hope** *for the* 21ˢᵗ **Century**

We the Young Peoples congratulate the United Nations for hanging in there for 50 years. Happy Birthday!

BUT WE ARE...

● disappointed that you couldn't have done more to save our generation from the scourge of war which has brought untold suffering to millions of us

● pleased that you created the Universal Declaration of Human Rights, but shocked by the failure of many governments to observe it

● thrilled by the existence of the International Court of Justice, but saddened by the way it is not being used

● delighted that the world has grown 17 times richer in the last 50 years, but appalled by the fact that so much of that wealth is controlled by so few

● infuriated by the insensitivity with which our governments have ignored the ancient wisdom of indigenous peoples, horrified by the slaughter and extinction of many beautiful species, and sickened by the ruin of the natural habitat of others

● worried about the spread of AIDS and other diseases

● terrified by the wide availability of drugs

● alarmed by the prospect of long-term unemployment

AND WE ARE...

● deeply concerned by the hopelessness and apathy these facts arouse in us

Left: *Maria Celeste Segui, 17, Argentina*

We *Therefore* **Resolve...**

to take the responsibility for our present and for the times to come. Our generation wants a chance "to save succeeding generations from the scourge of war." We live in this world and we see what's going on. We have ideas and energy to do something about the issues that bother us. We have things to say and we want to be heard!

However, up to now, the doors to the decision-making system have been closed to us. Maybe we haven't been knocking hard enough....

This book is a step in the right direction. It grew out of the United Nations of the Future Conferences we held in our different cities—from Freetown to Odessa to Los Angeles—where we came up with suggestions for making the UN a better, more efficient organization.

WE ARE DETERMINED TO...

- be open-minded and accepting of the world around us
- learn about human rights and join the organizations that directly promote them
- change some of our consumption habits and try to change the habits of those around us
- preserve the environment
- protect ourselves from sexually-transmitted and other diseases
- remember the traditional values of our cultures
- rekindle young people's interest in community activities

We want so many things to change, and we are ready to help make that happen. We will start in our own neighborhoods and reach out to the Big World. But for our voices to be heard by those in power, we will have to speak louder than ever before. And we see the United Nations as our channel. The UN already has the Youth Unit, but no youth in it!

If something bothers you, learn about it and help change it! That's what this book is all about.

GO FOR IT!

Above: *Isabel Albertini, 12, Argentina*

A Charter of Hope

CHAPTER ONE

The War to End All Wars

Before World War I (1914–1918) empires were built through military strength. War seemed glorious and to die for your country was heroic; poets rushed off to stain the soil of some foreign field with their blood! All that changed with World War I. In August 1914, everyone expected the war to be over by the end of the year. Instead, it became a four–year stalemate with the Central Powers and the Allies attacking and defending their lines of trenches with old-fashioned military strategies. Combined with increased firepower, these frontal attacks were suicide. There were more than 20 million casualties.

Following this terrible war, intense efforts were made to guarantee that it would not happen again. A hundred years earlier, the Congress of Vienna had tried to ensure that another Napoleon would not take over the world. Also, a Peace Palace had been opened in Holland in 1913, designed to settle national differences through an international court of law. Obviously, none of these things had worked. So a major part of the treaty that ended WWI (the Treaty of Versailles) was the establishment of a League of Nations.

Previous Pages
Left: *Markèta Vopatovà, 15, Czech Republic*
Right: *José Luis Bayer, 28, Chile*

Right: *Cecilia Weckström, 19, Finland*

This diary was "discovered" on an island by one of our contributors who said it was written by a French diplomat, Michel Mitterand. Our searches have revealed no record of him, but we liked the story. (Editors)

19 June 1917: Still now the war is raging. Destruction is at its zenith. Paris has been devoured by the smell of sulphur. Destruction has nearly crumbled this beautiful city into dust.

20 June 1917: It is with great pain that I am writing this page today. My father, a brave commander of France, has been killed in the battle fronts. I am grief-stricken, I am helpless. I saw him only a few weeks ago. A jolly and cheerful soul today lies still and cold somewhere in the battlefield—far away from us.

This moment I take a vow to strive hard and do something which will wipe away even the slightest stink of war from this earth and bring peace amongst the men all over the world so that no other child loses his father in a war—as I have. But I am still so young. Only time can tell whether my dream will be fulfilled.

13 July 1918: The war is over. But it has left behind scars of colossal destruction everywhere. The official number of those killed is about 20 million and those who are surviving are living a life even worse than those who are dead. Bulletins say that the social and economic conditions of Europe have been totally shattered.

The League of Nations

19 February 1919: I am feeling very happy today. Top leaders from the various countries of the world have joined hands and declared to form the "League of Nations"—a common platform for the people of every country of the world. The foremost objective is to end any kind of war between nations, and bring peace and integrity. Through the dark cloud hanging over all the sky I now feel a bright ray of sunlight bathing me all over....

—*Michel Mitterand's diary*

Geneva, with its one telephone line and one streetcar line, was not a likely place for the foundation of the League of Nations. However, 42 countries agreed on its establishment. Twenty-six of these were non-European. Germany was not allowed to join until 1926, and the USSR joined only after Germany left in 1934. Despite U.S. President Wilson's important role in forming the League, the U.S. Senate voted against joining out of fear that membership would involve the country in another war.

The two main aims of the League were to maintain peace through collective security, and to encourage international co-operation to solve economic and social problems. (Collective security means if one member state were attacked, all members would act to defend it using economic sanctions or military force.)

The main problems with the League were that action required a unanimous decision (including the transgressor if it was a member), and key states never joined.

The League's potential can be seen in its successful settlement (in favor of Finland) of the conflict between Sweden and Finland over the Aland islands. The League also dealt with prisoners of war marooned in Russia. Through the International Labor Organization, it improved working conditions in many parts of the world.

Like the UN that would succeed it, the organizational core of the League was the Council, the Assembly, and the Secretariat—all centered in Geneva. The Permanent Court of International Justice was set up in Holland.

The Great Depression contributed to the League's decline. Unemployment and falling standards of living in many countries gave power to extremist governments in Japan and Germany. They, along with Mussolini in Italy, openly flouted the League's rules. Japan invaded Manchuria, Hitler started his conquest of Europe, and Mussolini went after Abyssinia. Both Britain and France favored "appeasement." That is, they allowed the aggressors to get away with it. In the shattered post-war world, public opinion would not have approved a new war so soon after the last and appeasement was welcomed as a wise course of action.

Above:

José Maria Sert. Council Chamber ceiling, the Palace of Nations, Geneva

❝ *There must not be a balance of power but a community of power. Not organized rivalries but an organized peace. It must be a peace without victory. Victory would mean a peace forced upon a loser in humiliation. It would leave a bitter memory upon which terms of peace would rest, not permanently, but only as upon quicksand. Only a peace between equals can last!* **❞**

—Woodrow Wilson, 28th U. S. president

The *War* to *End* All Wars—*Again*

15 January 1939:

Adolf Hitler thinks that Germany is destined to rule the world. "Empires are made by the sword," he writes, "By theft and robbery, by brute force, we shall be the masters of the world!"

—*Michel Mitterand's diary*

In hindsight, it is difficult to understand why the League of Nations allowed Hitler to pursue his extensive campaign of violence and terror. Warmongers usually interpret appeasement as weakness, so Hitler was encouraged to go on and show the world that the League of Nations was nothing but a paper tiger. He considered his state supreme, and the interests of individuals were less important than the interests of the state. Encouraged by Japan's success in Manchuria, he set out to conquer Europe and finally plunged the entire world into total war.

World War II was much more complicated than WWI. Many more countries were involved. Major campaigns took place in the Pacific, the Far East, North Africa, the Soviet Union, the Atlantic, and in central and western Europe. Weapons and warfare had become much more sophisticated. Millions lost their lives and untold thousands were displaced. Economies were shattered. Great cultural treasures were lost and the psyches of nations were traumatized. Even today, our grandparents talk about "before the war" and "after the war."

Left: *Cecilia Weckström, 19, Finland*

Right: *Chihiro Tanaka, 17, Japan*

THOUGHTS FROM THE REGION OF AUSCHWITZ

It is incredible to live here in Krakow so close to the biggest crime of the century. Life goes on: we go to school, we go shopping, we have parties, but a few miles away lie the souls of millions of people murdered in the gas chambers.

Nobody knows why Hitler chose to make his biggest death camp here. Perhaps it was the railways. Perhaps because we had so many Jews in Krakow, but they were not only Jews in Auschwitz. My grandmother was there, and she was a Christian Polish woman. One day, she was supposed to be shot but the German soldier assigned to do it, was one she had cared for when he was sick. He had a heart and he saved her. Without him, I would not be sitting here writing this today.

If you go to Auschwitz today, there are no people, only echoes. You see the mountains of hair, the arm bands with the blue star that identified prisoners as Jewish. The spectacles, the shoes, the silent walls staring at you remind you of the pain and indignity that was suffered here. I find it horrible to look at my hand and think it was a hand not unlike mine that pulled the lever to release the gas that killed so many people all at once.

Who can those people have been?

—Magdalena Latosinska, 15, Poland

Steps to **UN**ity

The history of the United Nations begins in August 1941. World War II had just begun in earnest, and U.S. President Franklin Delano Roosevelt and British Prime Minister Winston Churchill held a top secret meeting "somewhere at sea." Together they drafted what became known as the Atlantic Charter. It outlined their plans to make a world of peace and security after the war was over. President Roosevelt suggested that all the states at war against the Axis Powers (Italy, Japan, Germany) should be called The United Nations.

T he goals of this 1941 meeting were confirmed at two further Summits in Moscow and Tehran during 1943, but the next crucial meeting took place at Dumbarton Oaks—a mansion in Washington, D.C. In the summer of 1944, delegates from the United States, Britain, the Soviet Union, and China met and drew up a blueprint for the new organization. France, still under occupation, did not take part. The discussions concentrated mostly on security.

In March of 1945, Churchill, Roosevelt and Joseph Stalin met at Yalta in the USSR where they agreed on the veto in the Security Council for the five major allied powers. The remaining articles of the Charter would be worked out at a conference to which all 51 countries that had declared war against the Axis would be invited.

Delegates from the future UN Member States arrived in San Francisco on April 25, 1945 by train. They had traveled slowly across the U.S. People paused to pray as their train passed, so great was the desire for peace. There was intense pressure from the press and public to make this conference a success. These delegates had a clear mission: to create an organization that would end forever the scourge of war.

Roosevelt, whose determination did much to make the United Nations a reality, died just before the conference

Right: *José Luis Bayer, 28, Chile*

opened. One of the first duties of the new U.S. president, Harry Truman, was to open the conference with these words: "At no time in history has there been a more important or necessary meeting than this. You are to be architects of the better world. In your hands rests our future....

"We who have lived through the torture and the tragedy of two world conflicts must realize the magnitude of the problem before us....

"This conference will devote its energies and its labors exclusively to the single

problem of setting up the organization essential to keep the peace. You are to write the fundamental charter."

It took two months to hammer out the details: 111 articles that spell out the UN's purpose and principles along with how to put them into practice. Australia campaigned to outlaw the veto, but the major powers would not take part in the organization unless they had one.

When it was all done, they met in the San Francisco Opera House on June 26, 1945 to sign it, solemnly and in turn. However, the United Nations was officially born on October 24, 1945. On this day, the Charter was ratified by a majority of the Member States and has been known ever since as UN Day.

THE UN CHARTER

The Charter remains one of history's great diplomatic successes. It is essentially unchanged: the only amendments have been to expand the Security Council and the Economic and Social Council. Amendment requires approval and ratification by the members of the UN including all the permanent members of the Security Council and is thus difficult to achieve.

Next pages
Left:
Paola Barresi, 19, Argentina

Right: *José Luis Bayer, 28, Chile*

24 OCTOBER 1945

Just now I have returned from the great function where the United Nations has come into existence. Today my promise has been fulfilled and I am closing my diary now and forever. My long cherished dream has been turned into a reality....

—Michel Mitterand's diary

A UNITED NATIONS

CHAPTER TWO

A *Trip* through UN **History**

Fifty years ago, the world was a lot different. There were less than two billion people, now there are close to six. We are generally wealthier; there is five times more money around now than there was in 1945. With computers and airplanes, we can move information and goods faster around the globe than ever before. (If passenger jets had been invented in 1945, the UN may not have been in New York, which is closer to Europe, but in San Francisco!) New technology lets us look deeper into the natural systems of the earth but there are still hazards: pollution, great poverty, and disease.

Through it all, the UN has been striving for positive change and to achieve cooperation in areas of common concern and shared destiny.

Right: *Jenny Pattinson, 16, United Kingdom*

1945
UN Charter signed in San Francisco.

1947
Churchill's Iron Curtain speech in Fulton, Missouri. Cold War begins.

1959
A declaration protecting the Rights of the Child is adopted by the General Assembly. It will be another thirty years before that declaration is given the force of law.

1960-65
44 newly independent nations become members of UN.

1961
UN Peace Enforcement action in Congo. Hammarskjold killed in a plane crash. U Thant named Secretary-General.

1962
Cuban missile crisis. UN helps to defuse superpower nuclear standoff.

1975
First International Women's Conference in Mexico City.

1980
Eradication of smallpox by WHO.

1981
Office of the United Nations High Commissioner for Refugees wins second Nobel Peace Prize for its assistance to Asian refugees.

1986
After Chernobyl, the International Atomic Energy Agency adopts two international conventions aiming to limit the risk of nuclear energy.

1995
50th Anniversary of the UN. World Social Summit in Copenhagen. World Conference on Women and Development in Beijing.

1994
UN Population Conference in Cairo.

1948
Universal Declaration of Human Rights accepted by the General Assembly. World Health Organization founded.

1956
Suez war starts. UN sends first UN peacekeeping troops to Egypt.

1954
The UN receives its first Nobel Peace Prize, awarded to the UNHCR for its work with European refugees.

1953
Trygve Lie resigns; Hammarskjöld appointed.

1965
UNICEF awarded the Nobel Peace Prize.

1969
The International Labor Organization wins the Nobel Peace Prize.

1974
The International Monetary System of fixed currency exchange rates (Bretton Woods) collapses, following global energy and food crisis. First Decade for Women announced.

1973
UN Environment Program is set up with Headquarters in Nairobi.

1972
The Stockholm Conference on Human Environment. Former Eastern Block countries (except Romania) boycott the conference as East Germany is not allowed to take part.

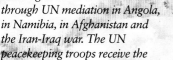

1988
Peace agreements reached through UN mediation in Angola, in Namibia, in Afghanistan and the Iran-Iraq war. The UN peacekeeping troops receive the Nobel Peace Prize.

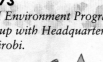

1989
Namibia achieves independence.

1990
World Summit for Children in New York with 71 heads of state.

1993
Eritrea gains independence from Ethiopia as a result of a referendum. Eritrea subsequently accepted as a member of the United Nations. Civil war ends in Mozambique under UN monitoring. UN supervises election in Cambodia after almost 15 years of bloody war.

1992
UN Conference on Environment and Development in Rio de Janeiro; results in Agenda 21. First Security Council summit held in New York with leaders from 15 member states; adopts Secretary-General's Agenda for Peace. UN Protection Force sent to former Yugoslavia to assist aid convoys, one of 18 peace missions the UN has set up since 1989.

1991
The UN establishes ceasefire in El Salvador after 10 years of civil war.

Getting a **Hand**le on the **UN**

How do you explain something as complex as the UN? Simple! Look at your hand: like the UN, it has "six major organs" (as they're called in UN-speak).

The **index finger** is the Security Council, pointing, ordering, and backing up its orders with diplomatic pressure, sanctions, and, sometimes, force.

The **thumb** is the General Assembly, applying pressure on behalf of the organization, but without the force of the Security Council.

The **middle finger** is the Economic and Social Council (ECOSOC), coordinating the social and economic work of the organization and its agencies (ILO, FAO, UNESCO, etc.). Some funds and programs like UNICEF and UNDP report directly to the General Assembly.

The **little finger** is the Secretariat with the Secretary-General at its head, providing services to the other organs and to Member States while urging and cajoling them to do what is important.

The **ring finger** is the International Court of Justice (ICJ), promoting obedience to international laws through its Court (a ring is a contract, defensible by law).

The Trusteeship Council rests in the **palm** of your hand. The UN Trust Territories are now all independent and self-governing so the work of this Council is formally suspended.

A **Hand**le on the **UN** Family

- **ILO:** International Labor Organization
- **FAO:** Food and Agriculture Organization
- **UNESCO:** UN Educational, Scientific, and Cultural Organization
- **WHO:** World Health Organization

- **WORLD BANK GROUP:**
  IBRD: International Bank for Reconstruction and Development (World Bank)
  DA: International Development Association
  IFC: International Finance Corporation
  IMF: International Monetary Fund

- **ICAO:** International Civil Aviation Organization
- **UPU:** Universal Postal Union
- **ITU:** International Telecommunications Union
- **WMO:** World Meterological Organization
- **IMO:** International Maritime Organization
- **WIPO:** World Intellectual Property Organization
- **FAD:** International Fund for Agricultural Development
- **UNIDO:** UN Industrial Development Organization

- **WFP:** World Food Program
- **ITC:** International Trade Center UNCTAD/GATT

- **Military Staff Committee**
- **Department of Peacekeeping Operations**

International Court of Justice

Economic and Social Council

Security Council

Secretariat

- **INSTRAW:** International Research and Training Institute for the Advancement of Women
- **UNCHS:** UN Center for Human Settlements
- **UNCTAD:** UN Conference on Trade and Development
- **UNDP:** UN Development Program
- **UNEP:** UN Environment Program
- **UNFPA:** UN Population Fund
- **UNHCR:** Office of the UN High Commissioner for Refugees
- **UNICEF:** UN Children's Fund
- **UNITAR:** UN Institute for Training and Research
- **UNU:** UN University
- **WFC:** World Food Council

General Assembly

Trusteeship Council

- **UNRWA:** UN Relief and Works Agency for the Palestine Refugees in the Near East

- **IAEA:** International Atomic Energy Agency

Left & Above: Cecilia Weckström, 19, Finland

UN *General Assembly:*
A Global **Talk Show**

Every member of the UN has a single vote in the General Assembly; small countries have as much right to speak as major world powers. Since almost every country on earth is a member of the UN, the resolutions adopted at its meetings give voice to a worldwide opinion. The resolutions, however, are only recommendations to countries.

Only when a security matter is deadlocked in the Security Council, and world peace is threatened, can the General Assembly step in and back up its decisions with force.

Though it might seem like it, the General Assembly is not a world parliament. It's a place where governments talk to each other and generate new ideas. The idea for the Rio Earth Summit came up as a General Assembly resolution, so did the Law of the Sea, which was raised by the small island country of Malta.

Right: *Chihiro Tanaka, 17, Japan*

26

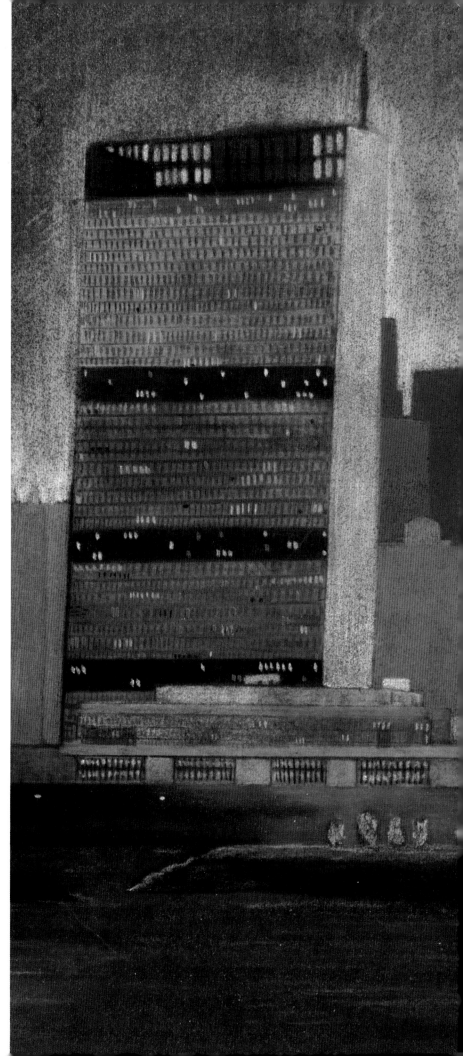

IN MARCH 1995, SEVERAL
OF US VISITED THE SECRETARIAT ON A
UNESCO/UN INTERNATIONAL
SCHOOL YOUTH ENCOUNTER
IN NEW YORK.

*Walking into the UN was the most
wonderful experience I ever had. I was
filled with curiosity, wanting to look
inside every nook and cranny and ask
about everything that I possibly could. I
was very impressed by the organization
inside and out, the flags arranged in
alphabetical order, the satellite dishes
receiving information from around the
world, 24-hours a day, the staff up late,
burning the midnight oil...I can imagine
why people so like to work for the UN. It
breathes excitement.*
　　　　　　—Omari Mtiga, 17, Tanzania

*I always had doubts about the UN. I saw
it as a huge bureaucracy with a lot of
boring, gray, serious characters. When I
walked in there, I did see some of them
but equally I found excited, energetic and
inspired ones. Rosario Green, Boutros-
Ghali's Assistant Secretary-General from
Mexico told me, "This is an organization
of people who work from their hearts for
ideals."*
　　　　　　—Danijela Zunec, 21, Croatia

Right: *Jenny Pattinson, 16, United Kingdom*

The **Secretariat**

Not only in the UN glass tower in New York but also in many offices around the world, UN Secretariat staff carry out decisions made by the other major organs. There are 25,000 staff members from 150 countries. They carry blue UN passports and are called "International Civil Servants." The buildings where they work are "International Territory" with their own security and pass systems.

Right: *Maria Soledad Bumbacher, 21, Argentina*

Below: *Nadya Rossokhina, 14, Russia*

T he work includes many things. For example, if the Security Council decides to send a peacekeeping force to a country, staff of the Department of Peacekeeping Operations get on the phone to Member States and ask them to lend the UN parts of their armed forces. If the General Assembly decides to hold a conference on population or an International Year of Youth, special staff are assigned to design and organize it.

Just handling the mail and translating the hundreds of documents generated into the six official UN languages (Arabic Chinese, English, French, Russian and Spanish) requires a huge staff. There have been complaints about unqualified staff taking on appointed jobs because of political pressures. The many brilliant and dedicated staff are forever coming up with new ideas about how to weed out the "deadwood" which can be a drag on the UN's effectiveness.

LIFE IN A GLASS TOWER

In 1945 Betty Teslenko went from being a flight attendant to being a verbatim reporter for the new UN. "I've never wanted another job. To sit and record the carefully thought-out words of brilliant, brilliant minds—that has been an honor for me. It never fails to give me a thrill when I get in a taxi and say 'United Nations, please!' People from every corner of the world pass me in the corridors—wonderful, brave people. UN staff are among the most idealistic in the world. I cannot imagine a more inspiring place to work."

"The Most Impossible Job on Earth"

This was how Trygve Lie described the UN's top job of Secretary-General. It's like being the president of a large, underfunded corporation, foreign minister to 185 countries at the same time, and nurse to the world's sorrows.

In 1945, many hoped that the job would go to one of the war-time heroes (Eisenhower, Churchill, even President Roosevelt briefly thought he might want the job) but the members quickly decided that, although the permanent members of the Security Council could veto the choice, none of their own citizens could ever be considered. Six people, all men, all diplomats, have held the post.

TRYGVE LIE
NORWAY, 1946–1952

He kept the organization together through the early years of the Cold War.

KURT WALDHEIM
AUSTRIA, 1972–1981

He built up the UN staff and opened a new office for the UN in Vienna.

DAG HAMMARSKJÖLD
SWEDEN, 1953–1961

His handling of the crises in Korea, Suez, and the Congo gave the UN great confidence. He was killed in a plane crash while on his way to negotiate with a rebel leader.

JAVIER PEREZ DE CUELLAR
PERU, 1982–1991

He presided while the UN grew in stature during the closing days of the Cold War.

U THANT
BURMA, 1961–1971

He kept the UN afloat during one of its most severe funding crises, and saw its membership double during his tenure.

BOUTROS BOUTROS-GHALI
EGYPT, 1992–

The first African Secretary-General, he is known as an activist who has, among other things, reorganized the Secretariat.

The *Security Council:*
The World's Bodyguard

Whenever a war breaks out anywhere in the world, people immediately want somebody to "do something!" That somebody is almost always the UN, and within the UN, it's the job of the Security Council. The UN's most powerful body, it's responsible for ending wars and keeping peace. Every peacekeeping operation you hear about is set up by, and takes its orders from, the UN Security Council.

The Council has fifteen members, ten of whom are elected for two year terms by the General Assembly. The other five, China, France, Russia, the United Kingdom and the United States, are permanent members and have the power to veto (veto means "I forbid" in Latin). This caused a lot of stalemates during the Cold War, but became less of a problem after it ended. It is generally agreed that the veto is the price the UN has to pay to keep the major powers as members.

In recent years, the Security Council has had a fair amount of success. Its officers helped negotiate the end of the Iran-Iraq war. Its forces helped secure free elections in Cambodia and Namibia. That success, along with the ending of the Cold War, has brought about an increase in the use of UN peacekeeping forces: 19 new operations have been set up by the Security Council since 1989. Some have been more successful than others.

Above: *Maria Soledad Bumbacher, 20, Argentina*

Right: *Anonymous, Costa Rica*

The *Struggle for Peace*

The UN cannot make peace; only governments can. Once there is peace, the UN soldiers can help keep it. However, many of today's wars are civil wars. Under Article II, 7 of the Charter, the UN is not supposed to intervene in domestic conflicts, but step in only when international security is endangered. Even then, the UN has to follow the guideline of "Peacekeeping with no combat capability." That is, "Keep neutral. Don't shoot unless you are shot at." These rules make the UN a spectator at most of the wars it would like to stop. Also, the UN has to be invited by both sides in order to have the privilege to watch. It is not designed to break up a fight.

Peacekeeping is new; there was nothing about it in the Charter. It was invented because it was needed during the Suez crisis. In the absence of a strong Military Staff Committee (that includes the military chiefs of the five permanent members), UN staff have been making up peacekeeping as they go along. Recently, the Secretary-General published the Agenda For Peace. After 35 years of peacekeeping, it defines what the UN can—and should—do in situations of conflict. It defines five key terms: preventive diplomacy, peace enforcement, peacemaking, peacekeeping and peace-building. Of these, perhaps the most important are the first and last: preventing a conflict before it ever breaks out and building the peace after the conflict is over.

Young people have been used throughout history by governments to fight their wars. Perhaps that could change too!

JANUARY 1995

In the beginning, people ran like hell
Whenever they heard that "tuff" from a
*   shell being fired.*
Then they learned to lie down and protect
*   their head.*
Now, they've stopped reacting at all.
All through the fall, they were firing one
*   shell an hour.*
Sometimes I found myself thinking:
"Come on and fire that shell then!"
And then I realized what I was asking for
*   is actually*
"Go ahead, kill somebody."

—photo and text by
Mia Björkqvist, 20, Finland

WHAT IS PEACE?

Peace is a gift that every person wishes to have. It is an absence of war and strife. Countries try to have peace and calmness, to hear the sound of the birds singing instead of hearing the tanks firing. Peace is tranquility, order, friendliness and security. Peace means prosperity. When a country has peace with its neighbors, it has the time to develop economically and spiritually. It has the time to create and provide opportunities for its people. Peace is a blessing and the absence of it is disaster. We all strive for peace, internal and external.

—Rami Ebbin, no age or country given

Left: *Roksalana Stošić, 13, Yugoslavia*

Blue *Helmets: Barefoot among the* **Scorpions**

In 1964, the UN sent a force to keep the peace between the Turkish Cypriot and Greek Cypriot communities.

Map: *Vajda Vatucte, 19, Lithuania*

**BRIGADIER MICHAEL HARBOTTLE
CHIEF OF STAFF, UNFICYP, 1964–68
INTERVIEWED BY
ADRIANNA KOE, 17, AUSTRALIA**

AK: Can you tell us something about the situation in Cyprus?

MH: *Between 1964 and 1968, a UN peacekeeping force brought the violence to an end and it did so without firing a single round of ammunition. This was achieved by the UN through its operational mandate which was not to use force. From the most junior soldier to the most senior officer, our primary responsibility was negotiation, conciliation and mediation.*

AK: Can you give us any examples of the kind of things you did?

MH: *Yes. There'd been a whole series of ethnic murders around Paphos, and people didn't dare move out of their villages, not even to work in their fields. The UN did a sort of shuttle diplomacy, going from village chief to village chief, asking them: "Do you intend using violence against your neighbor?" The universal answer was "No! But we're terrified they'll use violence against us." So we set up meetings between the chiefs of neighboring villages and asked them each, in the presence of a UN monitor, to say: "We do not intend to use violence against you." From then on, normal life returned to the villages.*

UNMIH
*United Nations
Mission in Haiti
since September 1993*

ONUSAL
*United Nations
Observer Mission
in El Salvador
since July 1991*

MINURSO
*United Nations Mission
for the Referendum in
Western Sahara
since July 1991*

PIECE-MAKING NOT PEACEMAKING

The UN came to Cyprus to ensure peace but all it has done is make our island in two pieces! UNFICYP does help us and our Turkish Cypriot neighbors, on various matters such as electricity, water supply, medical and mail services...."

—Marina Rafti and others, English School of Nicosia, Cyprus.

UNFICYP

United Nation Peacekeeping Force in Cyprus since June 1964

UNOMIG

United Nations Observer Mission in Georgia since August 1993

UNPROFOR

United Nations Protection Force in Bosnia-Herzegovina since March 1992

UNMOGIP

United Nations Military Observer group in India and Pakistan since January 1949

UNIFIL

United Nations Interim Force in the Lebanon since March 1978

UNOMUR

United Nations Observer Mission Uganda and Rwanda since June 1993

UNIKOM

United Nations Iraq-Kuwait Observation Mission since April 1991

UNAMIR

United Nations Mission in Rwanda since October 1993

UNOMIL

United Nations Observer Mission in Liberia since September 1993

UNAVEM

United Nations Angola Verification Missions since June 1991

Above: *Vajda Vatucte, 19, Lithuania*

An *Eagle* without **Claws!**

If your neighbor builds a fence around some of your land and pretends all of a sudden that it's his, what do you do? It's obvious: you take your neighbor to court. But if a state steals a piece of land, nobody does this. You get some tanks, some machine guns and you start a war. Why are states allowed to do this?

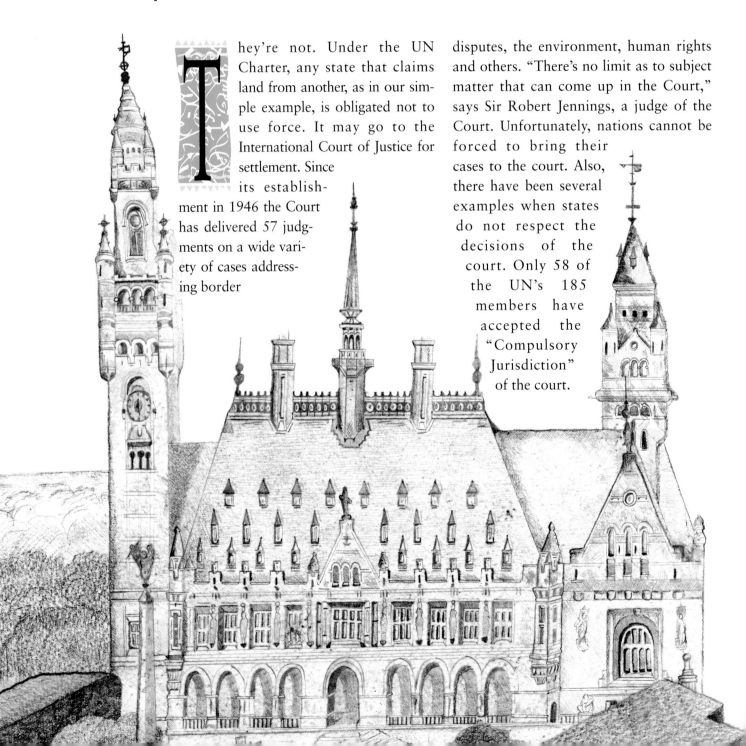

They're not. Under the UN Charter, any state that claims land from another, as in our simple example, is obligated not to use force. It may go to the International Court of Justice for settlement. Since its establishment in 1946 the Court has delivered 57 judgments on a wide variety of cases addressing border disputes, the environment, human rights and others. "There's no limit as to subject matter that can come up in the Court," says Sir Robert Jennings, a judge of the Court. Unfortunately, nations cannot be forced to bring their cases to the court. Also, there have been several examples when states do not respect the decisions of the court. Only 58 of the UN's 185 members have accepted the "Compulsory Jurisdiction" of the court.

The Permanent Court of International Justice was set up under the League of Nations in 1922. Its headquarters has been the Peace Palace in the Hague, Netherlands. Its work was taken over by the International Court of Justice under the United Nations.

Left: *Jenny Pattinson, 16, United Kingdom*

- Its main objective is to settle international disputes and to serve as advisory body on international matters.
- Only states can be taken to court and only states and no private person can accuse a state.
- Out of the 15 judges, three each are from Africa and Asia; two each are from Latin America and Eastern Europe; and five are from Western Europe, the U.S.A. and elsewhere.
- Judges are selected by the General Assembly for the quality of their training and judgment. Each serves a nine-year term. Each must be scrupulously independent in his or her decisions.

Above: *José Luis Bayer, 28, Chile*

❝ *The list of cases coming before the International Court has grown longer but it remains an under-used resource for the peaceful resolution of disputes. I urge once more that all Member States accept the general jurisdiction of the International Court. Greater reliance on its judgments would be an important contribution to peacemaking. It is therefore necessary to popularize, in the best sense of the term, international justice.* **❞**

—Boutros Boutros-Ghali, 1994

Trusteeship Council: *Midwife to* **Nations**

With the defeat of Germany, Italy, and Japan in WWII, an organization was needed to run their former colonies. Some were already ruled by the League of Nations Mandates Commission. The UN created the Trusteeship Council, to take over the Commission's work and to promote progress towards self-rule in these colonies.

An example of this was the British Mandate in Palestine which ended in the creation of the State of Israel in 1948. Other mandates for which the Trusteeship Council took responsibility included the Pacific islands of Micronesia, and former German and Italian colonies in Africa, such as Tanganyika, South West Africa, and Somaliland.

There were 11 Trust Territories in all. The last, Palau, achieved independence in November 1994 and became the UN's 185th member in December of the same year. The Trusteeship Council has since formally suspended its operations.

Mission accomplished!

DECOLONIZATION

One of the UN's greatest successes was the pressure it put on the major powers to transform their colonial empires into independent states. Since the Trusteeship

Right: *Maria Soledad Bumbacher, 20, Argentina*

Council supervised only the colonies of the defeated powers, in 1960 the General Assembly adopted a declaration to urge the speedy independence of all colonies and peoples. Since the adoption of the Declaration, some 60 countries have achieved independence. This is without doubt one of the UN's greatest

achievements, perhaps even more so because no one expected it to happen so quickly. Here is an example:

NAMIBIA

South Africa governed South West Africa as a mandate under an arrangement made in 1920 by the League of Nations Mandates Commission. After World War II, South Africa rejected the UN's request to place the territory under UN trusteeship. In 1966, the UN General Assembly voted to end South Africa's mandate but it took the people of Namibia, as they wished their country to be called, until 1990 to gain complete independence. With the UN's assistance, it held elections in 1989 to choose its first government.

ECONOMIC & SOCIAL COUNCIL

The Economic and Social Council (known as ECOSOC) was established by the Charter as the principle organ to coordinate the economic and social work of the United Nations, and the specialized agencies and institutions. ECOSOC discusses and makes recommendations on international economic, social, cultural, educational, health, and related matters. Fifty-four member states serve on the Council, each of whom are elected for a term of three years.

The six major organs—the General Assembly, the Security Council, ECOSOC, the Trusteeship Council, the International Court and the Secretariat—plus the specialized agencies and institutions are known collectively as the UN Family.

UN *Family*

When the UN was established in 1945, securing peace was the major concern. But the world's problems went far beyond military conflict. The UN identified the root causes of those conflicts as racism, violations of human rights, and social and economic divisions of the world.

Over the years and in response to many of these problems, the United Nations and its Member States established specialized agencies, programs, and funds to deal with these issues. These institutions are the tendons and muscles that articulate the UN hand. Aside from policy coordination through ECOSOC, it is a constant challenge for the UN to coordinate thousands of different agency employees working in different offices, in different time zones. Here are some of them:

UNICEF: UNITED NATIONS CHILDREN'S FUND

Below: *Andreanna Benitez, 12, Philippines*

One out of every three deaths in the world is the death of a child under the age of five. The UN believes that "mankind owes to the child the best it has to give" because children are the future. UNICEF works to ensure that happens in 128 of the world's countries, working with governments to provide services essential to the well-being of children: health, safe water, sanitation, nutrition and education.
Founded: 1946
Headquarters: New York, U.S.A.

ICAO: INTERNATIONAL CIVIL AVIATION ORGANIZATION

ICAO strives to ensure the orderly growth of international civil aviation.
Founded: 1944
Headquarters: Montreal, Canada

WHO: WORLD HEALTH ORGANIZATION

The goal of WHO is to lead all the peoples of the world to the highest possible level of health. One of its greatest successes was the Smallpox Eradication Program. In 1967, 10–15 million people had the disease but, after a 10-year campaign of education and vaccination, the last known case was detected in 1977 in Somalia. WHO is working with UNICEF to eradicate polio by the year 2000.
Founded: 1948
Headquarters: Geneva, Switzerland

WMO: WORLD METEOROLOGICAL ORGANIZATION

WMO is an authoritative scientific voice on atmospheric, environment, and climate change issues.
Founded: 1873
Headquarters: Geneva, Switzerland

ILO: INTERNATIONAL LABOR ORGANIZATION

The ILO works to promote social justice for workers everywhere. ILO's main aim is eventually to eradicate child labor. There are millions of children working in the world today—many of them in very dangerous conditions.

Founded: 1919
Headquarters: Geneva, Switzerland

IMO: INTERNATIONAL MARITIME ORGANIZATION

IMO promotes cooperation in international shipping.

Founded: 1948
Headquarters: London, England

UNESCO: UNITED NATIONS EDUCATIONAL, SCIENTIFIC, AND CULTURAL ORGANIZATION

UNESCO's constitution states: "Since war begins in the minds of people, it is in the minds of people that the defenses of peace must be constructed." This is why UNESCO promotes education worldwide, preserving the world's heritage and culture, improving access to communications and supporting social and scientific research.

Founded: 1946
Headquarters: Paris, France

"There are WHO health institutes in my home town. I remember the state we were in before WHO came, and I know that WHO has saved many of our lives. When a baby cries or a woman is waiting to deliver, they could die without WHO's help."

—Uda Giani, no age given, India

Right: *F. Sacco, no age given, Italy*

41

Above: *José Luis Bayer, 28, Chile*

Right: *Z. Halodova, 15, Russia*

Below: *Omar Bakry, 18, Egypt*

IAEA: INTERNATIONAL ATOMIC ENERGY AGENCY

The IAEA's purpose is to promote the peaceful uses of atomic energy. It supports atomic research for peace purposes, cooperates with state atomic agencies around the world, and monitors the treaty for nonproliferation of nuclear weapons signed by many, though not all, member states.

Founded: 1957
Headquarters: Vienna, Austria

FAO: FOOD AND AGRICULTURE ORGANIZATION

The aim of the FAO is to raise levels of nutrition and standards of living. It's concerned with seed production, soil protection, the sensible use of fertilizers, animal disease, and land reform.

Founded: 1945
Headquarters: Rome, Italy

WIPO: WORLD INTELLECTUAL PROPERTY ORGANIZATION

An idea, music, an invention—all are "intellectual property" which WIPO works to protect.

Founded: 1970
Headquarters: Geneva, Switzerland

ITU: International Telecommunications Union

Without the ITU, it would be more difficult to make overseas phone calls. It is the ITU that regulates the world's telephone and telegraph network by allocating international radio frequencies.

Founded: 1865

Headquarters: Geneva, Switzerland

UPU: Universal Postal Union

The UPU works to improve postal services and cooperation between postal authorities throughout the world.

Founded: 1874

Headquarters: Bern, Switzerland

UNHCR: Office of the United Nations High Commissioner for Refugees

"Refugee go home! He would if he could." (UNHCR poster)

There are over 20 million refugees in the world today. Most are women and children. All were forced into exile by intolerance and violence. They are from every race and religion. They come from every part of the globe. Their numbers grow each year as a sign of continuing upheaval around the world. A major part of UNHCR activities is to resettle and retrain refugees outside their countries of origin. But the office is primarily working to return refugees to their homelands.

Founded: 1951

Headquarters: Geneva, Switzerland

Shellings, Snowball Fights and Hard Work

Norwegian Bengt Halvorsen is a 47-year-old father of three and a UNHCR leader in Bosnia. He started in 1992, delivering Norwegian prefabricated houses. He was only supposed to work for six months, but has continued driving ever since. In January 1995, I traveled with Bengt and his team to several cities in Bosnia. Nine huge trucks were filled with basic necessities for about 60,000 refugees. Despite the pressure, the team regularly relaxes with coffee breaks, and has snowball fights while getting shelled.

Three weeks before, the whole convoy team had been held hostage. "The media made such a fuss about it," says Bengt, "but it was nothing compared to the troubles we faced last winter when one of our drivers was shot dead."

Bengt talked a lot about Nina, a 14-year-old orphan girl. He is determined to find a family for her in Norway. "I can't leave her here alone," he says. Most drivers last six months, maximum. Bengt has been doing it for three years, because of Nina. He says: "I can't think about finishing yet. For sure not before I get Nina to safety."

—Mia Björkqvist, 20, Finland

UNDP: UNITED NATIONS DEVELOPMENT PROGRAM

UNDP is the world's largest development assistance organization with 130 offices worldwide. It brings the expertise of the entire UN system as well as that of NGOs to bear on development projects in developing countries.
Founded: 1968
Headquarters: New York, U.S.A.

THE WORLD BANK

Right: *Sanjay Sinha, 13, India*

Below: *Edwin Riley, 21, U.S.A.*

The goal of the World Bank is to end poverty. It lends money at low interest to developing countries for big projects like roads, railways, and rural electrification, usually through governments.
Founded: 1944
Headquarters: Washington, D.C., U.S.A.

IMF: INTERNATIONAL MONETARY FUND

Before the collapse of the Bretton Woods exchange rate system in 1974, the job of the IMF was to manage the world's currencies. Today it works for the same goals, and strives to ensure the best conditions for economic growth.
Founded: 1945
Headquarters: Washington, D.C., U.S.A.

UNIDO: UNITED NATIONS INDUSTRIAL DEVELOPMENT ORGANIZATION

UNIDO promotes and accelerates the industrialization of developing countries.
Founded: 1966
Headquarters: Vienna, Austria

UNFPA: UNITED NATIONS FUND FOR POPULATION ACTIVITIES

The world's population increases by three people every second! UNFPA creates awareness of population problems and family planning. It also analyzes the impact of population growth on social, economic and environmental matters. In September 1994, the UN held a Global Conference on population in Cairo. It set targets for population programs worldwide.
Founded: 1969
Headquarters: New York, U.S.A.

IFAD: INTERNATIONAL FUND FOR AGRICULTURAL DEVELOPMENT

IFAD mobilizes resources to improve food production among low-income groups in developing countries.
Founded: 1977
Headquarters: Rome, Italy

The UN and Development

The World Bank, IMF, UNDP and other UN agencies and programs are all hustling to promote development. How do they work together?

In a number of ways. For example, say a developing country wants a cement factory. UNDP could give its government a million dollars to do a feasibility study to see if the numbers add up. If they do, the country would go to the World Bank and use the study to persuade it to invest $50 million to build the factory, with interest paid annually on the loan.

If the numbers don't add up, the UN loses a million—which is bad, but not as bad as losing $50 million. And by doing the study, the country learns about the reality of economic growth.

Clear? Well, it took us a while. The important thing to remember is that UN development grants are intended to help countries build their own economic capacity. These funds—though small in comparison—complement the hundreds of millions in loans from commercial banks, multinational corporations, and the Bretton Woods institutions. The UN thus cannot work miracles. But, in some developing countries, its assistance is a lifesaver.

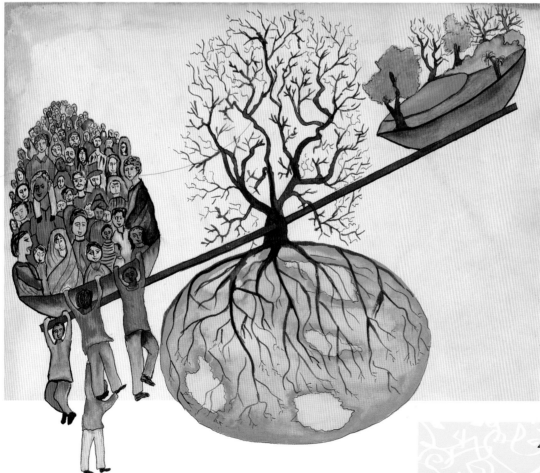

Sustainable Development:
Peace and **Plenty** Forever?

"There can be no flowering of development without the participation of the population; that requires human rights and democracy. Also, development is no longer merely a matter of economic policy. Social, educational and environmental facts must be a part of it.... Without development on the widest scale, the young will be restless, resentful, and unproductive."

—Boutros Boutros-Ghali, from a report on the work of the Organization

Top Right: *Yang Min, no age given, China*

Bottom Right: *Robert Arelano, no age given, Philippines*

Above: *Maria Soledad Bumbacher, 20, Argentina*

How does a country develop? How do we create prosperity and bring health, education, welfare, and a clean environment to all? Boutros-Ghali says: "A new and workable concept of development still eludes us." We asked the same question at the World Bank, and they freely admitted: "We don't know! Development is not an exact science."

But the UN has learned a few things—importantly, that building bridges and electrifying rural areas does not necessarily translate into "development." Also, you cannot cut down all your forests, sell the timber, and then throw a big party to show what a rich country you are. With all your trees gone, you will soon go bankrupt. The big news of the last decade is that we have figured out that economic growth must be "sustainable."

Sustainable development is about the present generation being prosperous without compromising the planet's abil-ity to deliver prosperity to future genera-tions. In other words, don't tear down the rain forest or puncture the ozone layer—future generations need them!

One of the greatest things the UN has done is to reorganize itself around the concept of sustainable development. There's a new Department of Sustainable Development; the agencies all have sus-tainable development officers. The whole idea of "development" is now linked to environmental preservation. The bottom line is: sustainable development is taking care of our future!

Sustainable development was born in a key report called, *Our Common Future*, prepared by a UN-apppointed, indepen-dent Commission in 1987. Brazil agreed to host a conference of UN Member States to discuss it, and suddenly the minds of politicians, governments, environmental and development NGOs, and people every-where focused on the Rio Earth Summit, which came up with the global agenda for the 21st century called Agenda 21.

UNCED 1992, *Rio de Janeiro*: *A Serious Effort to Save the* **World**

Agenda 21 is perhaps the most complex, most comprehensive document ever written on the world's problems. It is the foundation on which our future should be built. It is the blueprint for the world our children, grandchildren, and their children will inhabit.

I t looks at the human impact upon the natural world, and what we need to do to bring about prosperity and a clean environment for all. There is a children's edition of Agenda 21 called *Rescue Mission: Planet Earth*.

Agenda 21 reflects a consensus and commitment at the highest level to accelerate development while preserving the environment through cooperation between nations, and every sector of society within each nation. Including young people!

They agreed to it! They came down in their airplanes and stayed in their big hotels in Rio, and they signed the document. But what happened after that? Was it just a big media event? If Member States don't progress will the UN publicly single out those countries? It's easy to be cynical. If any government moves toward achieving the goals of sustainable development laid out at Rio, it will be a great step forward.

UN *and* NGOs: *Big Whale, Small Fish*

When I think about the UN and all the NGOs that work to make this world a better place each in its own way, I imagine a big whale and small fish. They all swim along together in the same direction. The big whale is strong, powerful, and impressive, but the small fish move more easily and quickly, sometimes getting more done.

—Danijela Zunec, 21, Croatia

N GO means NonGovernmental Organization and the UN works with hundreds of them. They are involved in activities as diverse as law, human rights, and disarmament. They often are not restrained by bureaucracies, nor accountable to governments. They're a bridge between governments and ordinary people.

It's because of their access and flexibility that NGOs often arrive on the scene of a tragedy before the UN, and that they can do more to protect individuals from Human Rights abuses than the UN. Also, because of their direct connection to the public, they can mobilize resources to deal with massive problems, like a sudden influx of war refugees.

Cora Weiss works across the street from the UN. She is on the NGO Committee for Disarmament. We asked her:

Why are NGOs so important?

The UN soon won't be able to afford its civil service. Increasingly, it will rely on NGOs for information and research. Also, the UN is a government organization whose members want the UN to protect their sovereignty and their borders. But problems don't stop at borders. Acid rain and refugees don't stop at borders. Human beings want to take care of things that governments cannot. NGOs offer them a way.

So what is the status of NGOs inside the UN ?

There are two types of NGO: those affiliated with ECOSOC, basically international ones, and those affiliated with the Department of Public Information, which are generally American. I believe that the UN is not doing enough to recognize the importance of either.

The spirit of volunteerism and internationalism united professional groups and like-minded citizens before the creation of the UN. Some suggested text for sections of the Charter.

Although the UN realized the importance of NGOs, for many years, it did not give them recognition. But during the 1992 UNCED conference, governments saw that NGOs did a lot of the groundwork. Partnerships were formed, NGO consul-

Below: *José Luis Bayer, 28, Chile*

tants were hired, and now many governments rely on NGOs for their expertise. Similar partnerships were built up around the Cairo Population conference and the Copenhagen World Summit for Social Development. UN Headquarters holds weekly briefings for its NGO affiliates and an annual conference each September.

NGOs inject the powerful force of "We the Peoples" into the UN. But they could do more; they are a sleeping lion waiting to awake and roar out truths. Youth NGOs are potentially the strongest.

Below: *Joanna Wasilewska, 15, Poland*

Next pages
Left: *Darine Spěváčkova, 13, Czech Republic*
Right: *José Luis Bayer, 28, Chile*

UN of the Future

CHAPTER THREE

In the Year 2024, a World without the UN

"Did you ever think how life would be now without the United Nations? I did. I saw a portrait of human beings still nursing the wounds of war, children, scarred, burned and bloodied, ground that screams of death, deceit and ignorance. I saw countries hanging on to what they think is right, fighting, proud of their pretense. I saw silent battles fought with money and power. I saw a world untouched by the word and action of the UN."

—*Portia Villanueva, 12, Philippines*

Right: *Cecilia Weckström, 19, Finland,* from an idea by *Dipesh Debnath, no age given, India*

Nightmare

Dear S.A.,

My dear son, I am writing this letter in the candlelight in my tent. It is raining outside, and I am alone here as all my fellow men died while fighting the blue-hair men. I don't know how to escape from here and there is no solution.

The world has been conquered by these men and they have destroyed our Flag of Peace. Do you remember? We had made it years ago when the UN had declared the end of war. We decided to organize our society in order to defend Peace, Human Rights, and Freedom in the world. We were 500 men from all nations, from different religions and races. We thought we were strong. Our flag was white and green. It looked like a star and a flower.

As a child, you liked it very much. You loved playing with it. Twenty years ago, all the nations had their own flower flags. I still have the photo which I took from the plane where you can see thousands of flags in every capital city of the world. Why didn't it last forever?

The blue-hair men have conquered and destroyed all nations. The flags, the houses, the factories, everything. Now the people are living in strange metal boxes, they are all wearing black uniforms; there are no schools, no libraries, no universities, hospitals, squares, streets, parks—nothing! Nothing beautiful left on the earth.

Here in my secret box, I have our last flag, these old photos, your last school report. I am leaving this letter here. I'll lock the box and hide it under our old tree. When you come back from your underground shelter, come here and you'll find these old things here.

You will be able to make a new flag, prepare new Peace Groups, and you will be able to win over the blue-hair men. Always remember: Believe in Life! Our underground schools are teaching the children how to believe in Life.

When you are 20 years old, you will be able to come back and defeat their cruel army.

My candle is finished.... Good-bye, my dear son, and good luck. And when you are sad, think of our flag, think of our songs, and be happy!

Love, your Dad

THE WORLD WITHOUT THE UN

Liar, murderer,
That's what man is now.
Fire, destruction,
Roaming this dying world.
Bombs, guns,
Are bought to stay alive.
Tired, weary,
My family are. Dead.

Gone, forever,
Trees are only memories.
Extinct, history,
Animals sit in museums.
A plant, a flower,
Then droop away and die.
Smog, smoke,
Pollution hangs. There.

Fighting, arguments,
Countries, constantly quarrel.
Conflict, corruption,
The next generation won't
*   follow.*
Cruelty, despair,
Drifts through the land.
Signaling, signaling,
Signaling man's end.
—Christine Hammond, no age
or country given

Another **Fifty** Years, Please!

"When I grew up in the '20s and '30s, the situation was abysmal. It was very obvious what was going to happen but there was not, at that point, any international way of dealing with aggressive governments. There was no human rights declaration; human rights were never mentioned in relation to the activities of Hitler. There was no serious attempt to approach economic problems on a global scale, and there was no talk of peacekeeping. So we have, to some extent, come somewhere...."

—Sir Brian Urquhart, former UN Under-Secretary, at the New York UN of the Future Conference

While writing this book, we received a lot of critical comments about the UN. Interestingly, no one said the UN should be disbanded. Why? Because it makes us feel safe. Or rather, it makes us feel very unsafe to think of the world without it. The UN does so much for us that we take for granted: letters reach us because of International Postal Union agreements; airplanes do not bump into each other because of UN-defined air corridors; books, TV shows, and scientific inventions can be sold around the world because of international copyright conventions supported by WIPO.

It is a flawed organization. Some of the stories of its need for increased competence are probably true, but still, the UN is a symbol of all that is good in human nature and the great promises of its Charter. It stands for the moral high ground staked out in the Declaration of Human Rights.

And it holds out the hope of a better future. Its staff is working to end poverty and hunger, cure disease, clean up slums, teach people to read, save children's lives, and peacefully reconcile nations in conflict.

And what you don't read about in newspapers is that it promotes the rights of the old, the disabled, and minorities throughout the world. The UN also validates the concerns of environmentalists, the idea of "sustainable development," and the fight to improve the status of women. It's now working for the cause of indigenous peoples and a special role for youth in government.

"Governments could, if they want, destroy the UN or make it ineffectual. But no power on earth could recreate it."

—George Schultz, former U.S. Secretary of State

Below: *Narongchai Sithiwatanaporn, no age given, Thailand*

Victim *of* Hope

Many of the young people who contributed to this book kept asking the UN to do what it is not empowered to do now. Why? Because we constantly see the despair of people on TV, in newspapers, sometimes even in our own communities and we want someone to do something. If our families, our towns, and our national governments don't do anything, the only place we feel we can turn to is the UN.

While preparing this book originally, we didn't plan to look at the future of the UN as closely as we have here. However, during the process, we kept asking why couldn't the UN do more of what we, and others, believe it should do. In order to answer this question—and to come up with some suggestions—we decided to hold a series of UN of the Future Conferences.

"I am a small girl aged eight years. I learned from my teachers that the beautiful Hiroshima was the first city to be destroyed by a big bomb. I feel safe that the United Nations is there to protect me today."

—Ana Ilmi, 8, India

Right: *Anonymous, Finland*

They killed my dad.
I want him back now.
I want freedom now.
UN, you are our only
 hope.
I have no security.
I have no peace.
I've got no shelter,
No warmth no
 health, no food.
All I have is myself
 and my mood.
My country is
 bombed,
My faith is gone.
It's a whirlwind of
 terror,
A hurricane of fear.
My family are
 fighting,
My friends are all
 dead.
I shall never see them.
I'm like a body with
 no head.
 —Vahaky Matossian,
 11, Armenia

UN *of the* **Future** *Conferences*

All over the world, we held UN of the Future Conferences; some big, some small, some lasting for weeks, some only an afternoon. At all of them, we discussed how this weird and wonderful organization founded 50 years ago could be stronger in the next century. We challenged the older generation, UN veterans and experts, to comment on our ideas. We now thank them for talking with us; their idealism was inspiring.

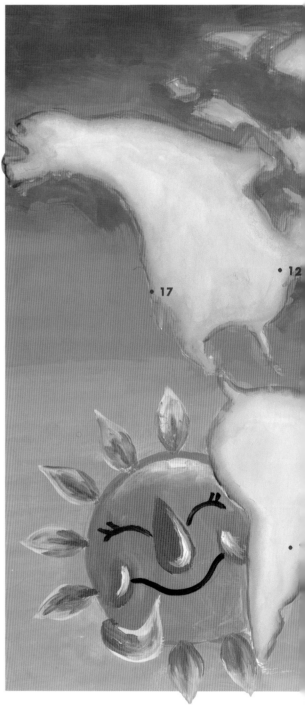

GENEVA

Sixty-five representatives from 21 UN of the Future Conferences met in Geneva for final brainstorming. It was incredible that all of us from so many different countries agreed on the major things we would like to change in the UN. Some of these hopes are:
- More Youth Access to the UN and much more youth activity, like a youth peacebuilding force;
- Use of the Internet and youth magazines to communicate to youth around the world what's happening in the UN;
- The International Court of Justice to be given more powers and regional membership of Security Council based on equal representation.

The following pages report on the other major concerns and proposals that came up at these UN of the Future Conferences.

Right: *Chihiro Tanaka, 17, Japan*

THE 21 CONFERENCES	
1. Where: Newport, England Participants: 35 When: March 9, 1995 2. Where: Freetown, Sierra Leone Participants: 150 When: March 13, 1995 3. Where: Olomouc, Czech Republic Participants: 60	When: February 22, 1995 4. Where: Odessa, Ukraine Participants: 60 When: February 2, 1995 5. Where: Bordeaux, France Participants: 140 When: February 15–17, 1995 6. Where: Manila, Philippines Participants: 50 When: November 11–

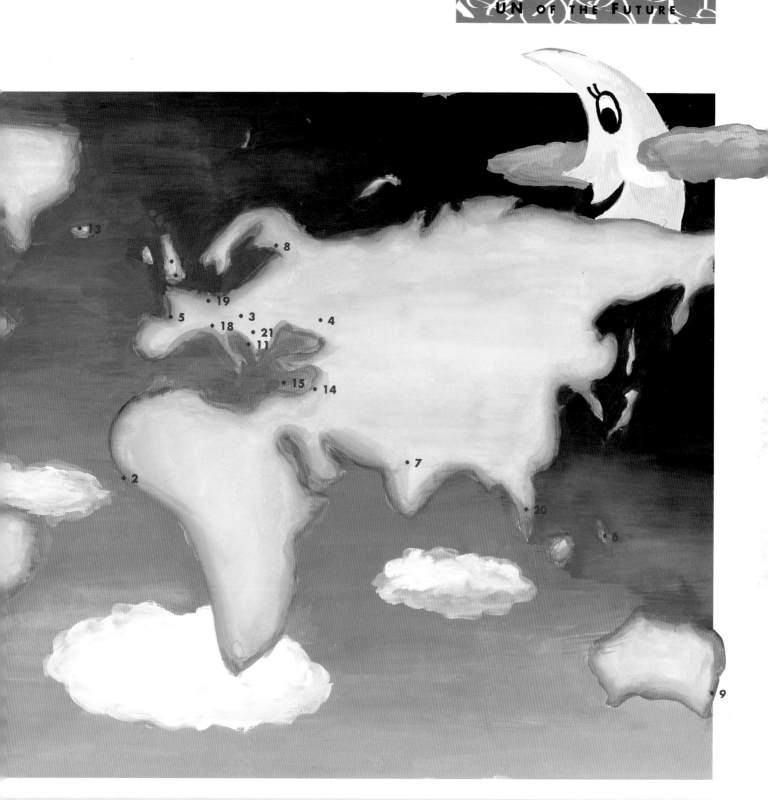

December 3, 1994
7. Where: Delhi, India
Participants: 50
When: February 10–11,
    1995
8. Where: Helsinki, Finland
Participants: 150
When: March 2, 1995
9. Where: Sydney, Australia
Participants: 40
When: March 12, 1995
10. Where: Cordoba,

Argentina
Participants: 400
When: March 11, 1995
11. Where: Belgrade,
    Yugoslavia
Participants: 50
When: March 11, 1995
12. Where: New York,
    U.S.A.
Participants: 35
When: March 6–13, 1995
13. Where: Reykjavik,

Iceland
Participants: 60
When: March 4, 1995
14. Where: Jerusalem, Israel
Participants: 15
When: March 1995
15. Where: Cyprus
Participants: North, 30;
    South, 15
When: March 1995
    (North & South)
16. Where: London, England

Participants: 100
When: February 10–12,
    1995
17. Where: Los Angeles,
    U.S.A.
Participants: 36
When: Janurary 17–19, 1995
18. Where: Geneva,
    Switzerland
Participants: 50
When: March 13, 1995
19. Where: Copenhagen,

Denmark
Participants: 200
When: March 9, 1995
20. Where: Bangkok,
    Thailand
Participants: 30
When: March 20, 1995
21. Where: Pristina,
    Yugoslavia
Participants: 30
When: March 16, 1995

Breaking *the* Chains

Human rights was a top priority for most UN of the Future Conferences and most of us wanted to find ways for the UN to punish the abusers. But first, some background:

In 1948, the UN adopted the Universal Declaration of Human Rights, one of its first and most important documents. It sets the standard of protection of individual citizens from abuse, and for his or her fundamental needs. Its first article says that "all people are born free and equal in dignity and rights." No matter what your nationality, ethnicity, religion, race, gender, age, or property, you have the right to freedom from slavery, freedom from torture, a fair trial, freedom of thought, religion and expression, as well as the right to education, to an adequate standard of living, to work, to form political parties and participate in government, and join a trade union.

All 185 members of the UN have signed this Declaration. But we still have wars and discrimination—so much abuse of these rights. Why is that so?

The Universal Declaration is a standard, but it is not law. On the next page, Solzhenitsyn makes the same mistake that many of us made: the UN cannot enforce any rules or laws. Member States do that. The UN only carries out the wishes of its members. If the members do not wish the UN to enforce these rights, it cannot, no matter how much its staff may want to.

All the UN can do, and has done over the years, is to pressure members who do not respect these rights. It held a World Conference on Human Rights in 1993 which upgraded the status of the Human Rights Commission within the UN system. It collects information on rights abuses and sends special "rapporteurs" to investigate cases. To prosecute war crimes, the UN has begun the difficult process of creating International War Crimes Tribunals.

SO WHAT CAN YOUTH DO?

First, read the Declaration; learn your rights and help defend them. Second, ask questions. Third, speak with your governments. How can the UN remain neutral in the face of aggression? The answer lies in Chapter II, Clause 7 of the Charter which forbids the UN from getting involved in the internal affairs of Member States. Many of us felt the time had come to change this. We believe the UN should be able to discipline its members who abuse their citizens.

The UN already puts pressure on governments, but the Helsinki UN of the Future Conference felt it should do more: A new human rights organization, staffed and run by young people, should be set up at the grassroots level. It could have a rapid response force to look into abuse and bring representatives of accused governments immediately before an International Criminal Court. It could lobby governments to change the Charter to allow the UN to prosecute human rights abusers.

Right: *Vajda Vaitucte, 19, Lithuania*

Far Right: *Avelina Sloboda, 15, no country given*

"The best document the UN put out in all its twenty-five years was the Declaration of Human Rights, yet the UN did not endeavor to make endorsement of it an obligatory condition of membership. Thus it left ordinary people at the mercy of governments often not of their choosing."
—Aleksandr Solzhenitsyn, Russian writer

Children's *Rights*

According to UN statistics, by the year 2000, there will be over 6,000,000,000 people on the earth. If we were all to join hands, the line would stretch to the moon sixteen times! More than half those people will be young people under 18. People like us.

In November 1989, the Convention on the Rights of the Child was adopted by the UN General Assembly. It has now been signed by more UN Member States than any other Human Rights Convention. It grants children the right to education, food, and health care; prevents them from being used in military forces until they are 15; allows them to participate in making decisions that affect them; and allows them to complain, in person, if they feel their rights are being abused.

The last one is an important right: every UN of the Future Conference commented on it, using it as a justification for youth to be more involved in the work of the UN. That right is reaffirmed in Agenda 21, as well as in the Declaration of the World Summit for Children, which states that governments should "seek partnerships, especially with children, to achieve their goals."

However, kids are being deprived of their rights daily, often with government cooperation. Around the world, over 50 million children work in unsafe and unhealthy conditions. 120 million between the ages of six and eleven receive little or no education. Some 3.5 million die each year of diseases which could be prevented or cured.... The list goes on and on. Why do governments sometimes sign these important-sounding declarations, then do so little to implement them?

A children's rights committee has been set up in Geneva which investigates any appeals sent to it by kids (18 and under) who feel their rights have been abused. We urge you to learn more about your rights and, if they are being abused, to write to this committee. Here is its address:

Committee on Children's Rights
Center for Human Rights
Palais des Nations
CH–1211 Geneva, Switzerland.

Right: *Cecilia Weckström, 19, Finland*

Far Right: *Eun Ju Lee, 11, Guam*

One child dies,
Your world has ceased to turn.
Ten children die,
The television has broadcast it.
A thousand children die,
We're getting used to it.

—Silvio, 13, France

Don't You **Dare** Use Military Force!

At the UN of the Future Conferences, the loudest calls for reform came from those whose countries were in the grip of war. In 1945, the United Nations was supposed to guarantee not that there would be no more conflict but that those conflicts would be settled peacefully. It hasn't happened. All conferences wanted the UN of the future to be better at preventing wars. As adult experts consistently reminded us, this is difficult, if not impossible—but at least they agree that we owe it to all those suffering the agonies of war to try.

PROPOSAL ONE:
A UN VOLUNTEER PEACE SERVICE

All UN of the Future Conferences endorsed the idea of a UN Standing Volunteer Force, under the command of the Security Council, consisting of volunteer soldiers, and available to deal with any problem.

In New York, they proposed: "We believe that young people's interests are served better by international service for peace rather than national military service." We feel that today's system, with the UN begging for troops and funding every time there's a crisis, is ridiculous! Member States always set conditions: "We'll only go to this place. How much will you pay? Our general must be in charge!" No nation would run its own army this way. Why should members expect it of the UN?

PROPOSAL TWO:
REFORM THE SECURITY COUNCIL

Right: *Anna Kasatkina, 14, Russia*

The world has changed fundamentally in the last fifty years, but the composition of

the Council still represents the world as it was after World War II. All our conferences discussed the idea of other countries getting a permanent seat plus veto powers, but there was more excitement for regional seats: "There could be regional Security Councils. Organizations like the European Union or Organization of African Unity could have Security bodies, linked to the central UN Security Council. Each region would have a permanent seat, shifting responsibility for security from the national to the regional level. We endorse the idea of a single European seat."(From the Bordeaux conference)

PROPOSAL THREE:
UN WORLD GOVERNMENT?

In 1945, many people believed that the

UN would quickly become a Federal World Government. Several conferences endorsed the idea, even though they recognized it might not work out: "In modern society a person can, and even must, feel himself a citizen of the world, sharing responsibility for everything happening on earth." (From the Odessa conference)

As a first step, many have called for a People's Assembly, directly elected by the people in a worldwide election. But who would pay for it? What would it do? What power would it have? And would anybody listen to it?

The Commission on Global Governance, a group looking at how our world should be governed in the 21st Century, endorsed the idea of a People's Assembly. It also called for a place within the UN where "individuals can petition to redress wrongs that could imperil their security"—something like a 24-hour hotline to a Court of Human Rights. "It would be a high-level panel of five to seven persons independent of governments, appointed by the Secretary General to hold in trust the security of people."

Is it possible for our generation not just to reform the UN, but to rebuild it as a democratic world government? We're not entirely sure, but it's worth trying.

"Idealism is the best form of realism because if you don't have some ideals, you don't have objectives, and if you don't have objectives, you're dead in the water. You're not going to move anywhere."

—Sir Brian Urquhart

Help Us

It's hard to know what more the UN can "do" for needy countries. The UN can only deliver as much aid as it can persuade its member governments to give. Some governments think primarily of enriching themselves not their people, or they spend so much on weapons that they don't have enough money left for education or health care. And putting pressure on them doesn't always work.

But we must all keep trying....

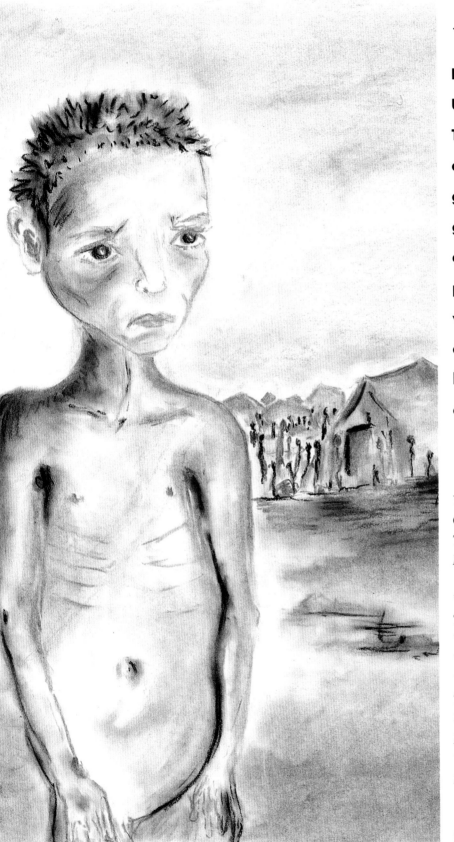

You were born in 1945,
Charged with fostering a world at peace
Through a new world order.
But Africa is left alone,
    crying alone.
We ask: has the United Nations filled
The strong room of hopes that it built in us?
What about the slums of Africa?
What about the deaths from ravishing famine?
What about the tyrant, power-drunk army boys
That kill us and start a war for personal glory?
United Nations! We salute thee!
But now,
Wake up from your slumber
Do something for Africa!
                        —a 19-year-old African youth

Left: *Camilla Ilmoni, 16, Finland*

UN **Do Something**

But what? We considered this question and came up with some answers:

Freetown, Sierra Leone: Stop the war! There can be no further development without peace!

Helsinki, Finland: Empower and educate women, and urge the UN to do more for their independence.

Delhi, India: Write off debt! (Developing countries are paying more in interest to the developed world than they are receiving from it—over $150 billion between 1982 and 1989! This is more than the U.S. gave to Europe after World War II with the Marshall Plan!)

AND THERE WERE OTHER IDEAS:

Below: *Oguzhan Oguz, no age given, Turkey*

An Economic Security Council: Poverty can kill as well as a bullet. The UN needs an ESC to deal with large-scale unemployment, mass poverty, ecological disaster, and the collapse of food supplies. It could consist of the G-7 countries (Canada, France, Germany, Italy, Japan, United Kingdom, United States) plus China, India and regional representatives. No country would have a veto. The New York UN of the Future Conference suggested that the ESC could merge with the existing Security Council so that all aspects of human security could be dealt with by one single, powerful authority.

Empower developing countries: End the culture of dependency! Don't allow the continued growth of an underclass of nations that survive on handouts. Encourage private investment. Promote "Trade not Aid"; create a fair trading system for developing countries with incentives, like easy access to appropriate new technology.

Promote people-to-people connections: There were many ideas like this, such as links between schools in the developed and the developing world. UNESCO has a plan for this which should be vigorously supported.

AND FOR MANY OF US:

Consume less: Conspicuous consumption doesn't always help us enjoy life more, and it's a problem. If people in the developed world could be satisfied with less, development problems could be massively reduced.

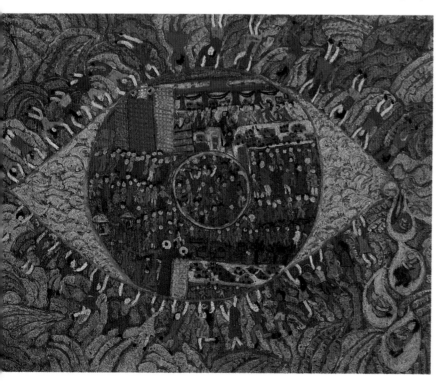

Efficiency

And there's more the UN can do:

Right: *Stamps*
© *United Nations*

Far Right: *Gotaro Ohara, no age given, Japan*

Get the finest staff in the world!: We feel it is vital that the world's most important organization be staffed by the best possible talent. The UN could:
• Hold competitive examinations for every job so that the best possible candidates may be recruited;
• End government pressure for certain positions as well as some restrictions for others;
• Establish a UN Staff College to train top quality UN civil servants.
Everybody we talked to told us that no Member State would ever agree to most of this, but we would like them to try!

UN Finance Reform: During the making of this book a lot was said to us about the UN's shortage of funds and the fact that the UN's budget is less than the budget of the New York City Police Department. The entire UN family's budget is about $10.5 billion per year—or about $1.90 per person on the planet! For a secure, environmentally clean world, with health, food, and education for all, we believe that many people could give $1.90, or maybe even $2.00 but the UN has no power to raise taxes directly from the world's citizens—it cannot even borrow funds from a bank.
• Tax the arms trade. The Member States want to control UN finances, but this should stop. We propose a UN tax on arms trading. Then the compa-

nies and countries who have the biggest stake in trading in arms would also make the greatest investment in UN peacekeeping operations—which have to mop up the messes caused by the arms they sell.
We also endorse other tax suggestions from the Commission for Global Governance:
• Tax everything that emits carbon into the atmosphere (which contributes to global warming);
• Tax global currency speculation, so when a huge investor makes a billion on varying exchange rates, a percentage of it goes to the UN;
• Charge a fee for parking satellites in space;
• Charge for the use of resources in Antarctica;
• Tax airline tickets for the use of international airspace;
• Tax tanker-ship traffic for the use of international shipping lanes.
By raising its own funds, the UN could rapidly become a much stronger, more independent and more effective organization. We propose that Member States have faith in the organization and allow it to do some of these things.

66

The UN's Image

Every one of our UN of the Future Conferences commented on the poor image the UN has among young people. Many of them hadn't heard of the UN, and often those who had heard of it had a negative opinion.

The media generally reports only on the bad stuff, the failures, the tragedies. Young people pick up on this; many feel hostile toward the UN. The UN has to do a better job of selling its good side. Only if the UN reaches out will citizens want to be a part of the great work that the UN is trying to do.

Privatize the UN? Would privatization benefit the UN? We think so. Better media relations, better publications, better merchandise—all the kinds of things that the entertainment companies make fortunes on could increase the popularity of the UN. With that in mind, we make the following recommendations:

- Let public relations companies bid for the privilege of promoting the UN and licensing it worldwide! Kids would see the UN logo on lunchboxes, pencils, and toothbrushes. Use the profits to finance development projects.
- Contract out national defense to a UN Security Company. It would work like an insurance company: rather than having its own army, a country would depend on the "UN Security Force." It would be financed by national premiums, trained in special UN camps, and available at a moment's notice. This idea was discussed at the Reykjavik conference. Eventually, national armies would be unnecessary.

Privatization can often go too far, but a little business sense has worked wonders for many previously government-owned enterprises. The UN has already privatized some of its operations. Maybe it should do more!

The UN should have a new look, that is what I think. Most countries desire a UN renewal. A more democratic UN? Perhaps—but I am too young to spell out the details.

—Henry Maria Mwamanenge, 11, India

Right: *Viola Caretti, 14, Italy*

Garden *for* Us

"Humankind has not woven the web of life. We are but one thread within it. Whatever we do to the web, we do to ourselves. All things are bound together. All things connect. Whatever befalls the Earth befalls also the children of the Earth."

—attributed to Chief Sealth, 1855

Everything impacts our environment, and producing anything uses up resources and energy. Developed countries with small populations use more than half of the world's energy resources. Developing countries with larger populations use a fraction of the energy resources. It doesn't sound right, does it? Yet, the goal isn't to bring the developing world to the consumption levels of the developed world, but rather to balance the situation. Back to sustainable development.

One of the suggestions from Rio was to convert the UN Trusteeship Council into an Environmental Security Council. Perhaps it could share responsibilities or merge with our proposed Economic Security Council.

Our UN of the Future Conferences focused on strengthening environmental education; raising the profile of the UN Environment Program (UNEP: an important organization which monitors environmental issues); levying "green taxes" to encourage eco-friendly consumer spending; and creating more binding international regulations to force governments, corporations, and individuals to live environmentally sustainable lifestyles.

Right: *Anonymous, Russia*

DOES IT MATTER?

*Every day children and grown-ups die
    from hunger and thirst.
Does it matter?
We say while we vomit
    to stay thin.*

*Every day, people are shot and
    killed in war.
Does it matter?
We say while shooting each other
    with our toy guns.*

*Every day animals are killed
    for science.
Does it matter?
We say as we smear lipstick
    on our mouths to look beautiful.*

*Every day the ozone layer
    gets thinner.
Does it matter?
We say while spraying ourselves
    with deodorant and perfume.*

*Every day trees are
    chopped down in the rain forest.
Does it matter?
We say while tossing out the paper
    we just used.*

*Every day there are children
    unable to get an education.
Does it matter?
We say while claiming to have a sore throat
    in order to skip school.*

*Every day there seems to be
    a little less of this world.
Does it matter?*

—Benedicte Fikseaunet, 14, Norway

In **Their** Opinion

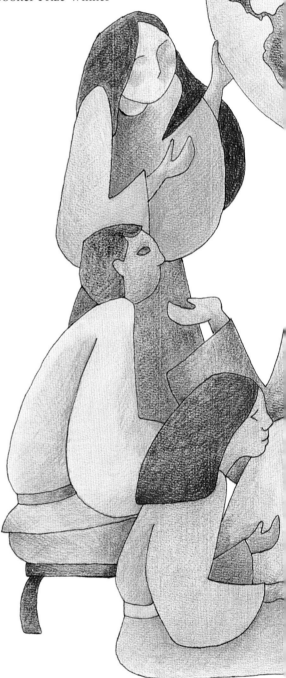

"In each capital I visit I am taken to the monument of the unknown solidier, but I have never been shown a monument to the unknown peacemaker."
—U Thant, former Secretary-General

"The trouble with the UN is not that it has failed, but that it has not been bold enough. It is not independent enough. And it has lost sight of the clarity of its great original dream."
—Ben Okri, Author & Booker Prize Winner

"I believe the UN should be much smaller organizationally, and vastly more effective in enforcing its resolutions. I believe it should maintain a standing army raised by member states which should be empowered to take preemptive action where gross infringements of human rights and gross acts of brutality are foreseen."
—John le Carré, Author, The Spy Who Came in from the Cold

"Why should we wait for another world war to devise a better planetary system than the UN? Let us be sensible and either improve the UN or create a better world organization right away."
—Robert Muller, Author, My Testament to the UN, and former Under-Secretary-General

"The UN needs a tremendous expansion. The world needs a new generation Charter."
—Harold Stassen, Signatory of the UN Charter, United States of America

"The world is chaotic, but without the United Nations it would be a complete disaster."
—Robert Muller

Right: Anonymous

Next Pages
Left: Fern Bernays, 17, United Kingdom
Right: José Luis Bayer, 28, Chile

"The United Nations is not an organization designed to take mankind to heaven, but rather to save it from hell."
—Dag Hammarskjöld, former Secretary-General

"We believe that the UN remains the essential center for harmonizing the actions of the nations. That is why reform of the UN system is a central part of the responses we suggest to the challenge of global governance. We agree with the External Affairs Committee of the Canadian House of Commons that the world needs a center and some confidence that the center is holding; the UN is the only credible candidate."

—From *Our Global Neighborhood*, the report from the Commission on Global Governance

"There is nothing wrong with the UN, except its governments."
—Lord Caradon, former Representative to the UN, United Kingdom

"The General Assembly of the UN is not, and could never be, a democratic organization."
—Richard Gott, Journalist, The Guardian, London

QUESTION:
"The world today is so violent, and the guilty ones never seem to be punished. How can we expect from young people to behave any different but violent? They don't know the other way."

—Mahbub ul Haq, Editor, UN Human Development Report

ANSWER:
"If we can teach the blind to sense the colors, if we can teach the deaf to sense the sounds, then I am sure we can teach the violent about peace as well."

—Rosario Green, Special Political Advisor to the Secretary-General

CHAPTER FOUR

KIDS HAVE POWER

Young people have long been achieving incredible things. Look at this painting, created by a 15-year-old Peruvian in the middle of the rain forest! He's not alone. Kids throughout the world have helped lead the environmental movement, composed great symphonies, led revolutions, survived astonishing hardship even sometimes led nations (Joan of Arc led France to freedom when she was only 16!).

Yet many kids feel overwhelmed by the complexities of the world's problems. Ivan from Romania is the same age Joan of Arc was when she led France. He wrote to us: "I am surprised that you ask our advice about the UN's future. We are only children. Keys are in the hands of powerful men, statesmen, governments. Those who have a lot of money. What can children do if the destiny of humanity is threatened?"

OUR ANSWER IS: A LOT.

Em**power**ment

Every UN of the Future Conference agreed: young people want their ideas heard! The call in Geneva was for a Youth Assembly, a young people's division at the United Nations. Well, it exists already. It's called the UN Youth Unit. Ever heard of it? Neither had we. A group of us went to investigate, hoping to find hordes of young people, bursting with energy. There were none. The Youth Unit has no youth in it!

Part of the problem is the way it's set up. It's supposed to be a "report writing body." But we don't want reports, we need *action*. Let's try to *do* something new!

Partnership

The greatest gifts the UN can give to us are legitimacy and a hotline to our governments. It did it for women; it did it for indigenous peoples. It can do it for us! Then the idea of young people's participation might be recognized and accepted by those in power. With Agenda 21 and the Convention on the Rights of the Child, it has already started.

The UN of the Future Conference in the Philippines suggested a basic change: add the word "children" to the preamble of the Charter, so that it reads: "...in the equal rights of men, women, and children...." It may not seem like much, but it would remind everyone who reads that inspiring document that children (defined by the UN as people under 18) are a unique and significant part of society.

The UN has many youth activities (UNESCO Clubs and associated schools, UNEP Youth Forums, the UNICEF Youth NGO Committee, and the Youth Unit), but in none of them is there a sense—yet—of genuine partnership with young people.

The idea of partnership with young people is already gaining ground and producing interesting results, like this book. This could not have been done without the help of our teachers, adults within the UN, our clubs, historical advisors, designers and printers. It's been great working together as equals. There are many other examples:

- The Australian UN Youth Association (UNYA) has been built up by young people in partnership with the adult UN Association and a teacher organization. It runs a conference every year with hundreds of young people. The Australian government takes its resolutions very seriously.
- There are Model United Nations (MUN), elaborate simulations of UN activity where young people take on the roles of diplomats searching for solutions to real problems. 100,000 young people take part in MUNs every year.

ACTION!

But if kids don't go home from these meetings and do something, what's the point? We don't need just more conferences. There's so much work to do—that's why this plan of action needs you, needs all of us. For example, if we believe in human rights, we must accept responsibility for helping to monitor them. If you live in an area affected by drug abuse, or there's a big polluting factory right outside your window, or you are wasting resources, be part of the solution—otherwise you are part of the problem. It's easy to sit down and write all the reasons why somebody else should act, but nothing happens that way.

Get support from other people. Start talking about the issues and you'll find many who think like you, but didn't say anything until you did. Together, you can put pressure on whomever is responsible: consumers, businesses, governments.

Left: *Paola Barresi, 19, Argentina*

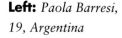

"Never doubt that a small group of committed people can change the world. Indeed it's the only thing that ever has."
—Margaret Mead, from *Only One Earth*

LEARN ABOUT THE UN

Every UN of the Future Conference report stated how little young people actually know about the UN. It goes both ways. The UN should talk directly with us, instead of through adult "youth experts."

"We don't want merely to learn facts about the UN in schools," said one report, "We want active, hands-on participation with the UN: learning by doing." That's more than just shaking a collection can for UNICEF!

HOW? REVAMP THE YOUTH PROGRAM

We see the UN Youth Unit as one of our channels. Why invent something new when it exists already? The UN Member States have agreed to it and have given it an annual budget. All it needs is new energy, a new role. And us!

A "youth-full" Youth Unit could be run on the model outlined here of young people in partnership, and it could begin action on the local, national, and global level. It could be the network hub, with young people working there, generating and exchanging ideas, energy, and information, and spreading it all out to young activists around the world— and throughout the UN system. It could link young people via the Internet and other communication services—a digital youth network, connecting millions of young people. A "virtual UN" in cyberspace is within our grasp; creating it would move the UN into the 21st century, and make it real to us.

A WORLD YOUTH SERVICE

This was proposed by many UN of the Future Conferences. Many of us face a year or two of national military service. Most of us want to serve, but it would be great to serve in a global force, working with young people of different nations.

The Helsinki conference proposed a human rights youth monitoring force; Freetown and New York proposed a new peace-building, peace-enhancing service—instead of "Blue Helmet" soldiers, the "Blue Jeans." The Blue Jeans could go to troubled areas to work with the local young people to avoid conflict, or to help heal the scars of war after a ceasefire is signed.

We know there can be problems with volunteers of our age: those good-hearted know-nothings who get in the way are more of a problem than a help. That's why we must organize in partnership with adults. Such a service could be an excellent transition from school to the working world, or from school to college. Service could be part of every kid's education. We feel simply that it should be global service—the Blue Jeans.

Left: *Anna Akcenoba, 16, no country given*

Long Live *the UN!*

We love the idea of the UN. We love the idea that it should become a global government occupying the moral high ground. We want to be part of a global family and live in a global village. And with communication through TV and the Internet, many of us feel we already do. There's so much more the UN might do if our generation could get our governments really behind us. The UN could be:

- the World's Supreme Court to which we, the peoples, could appeal over the heads of our governments;
- a Global Peace Force, protecting us from the ravages of civil and international war;
- the guarantor of Global EcoSecurity for all living beings;
- the manager of our natural resources, ensuring that no living being goes to sleep hungry;
- a global communication service, etc.

It could be all of these things—and we, the Young People, want to help make it so.

Below and Far Right: *Edwin Riley, 21, U.S.A.*

OVER TO YOU!

The UN is already working to get you involved in its transformation and connect you to its work. For its fiftieth anniversary, it is issuing a Global Passport to the Future to every young person who requests one.

The Passport says: "As the world changes, so does the United Nations. You are part of that change. As a citizen of the future, you belong to the United Nations. And as an organization for the future, the United Nations belongs to you."

We urge you to get one. If you can't find a United Nations Association in your telephone book, then write to Rescue Mission Headquarters and they will help you. Then, read the Declaration which asks you to pledge things like:

- "I will seek to understand the lives of other people, to respect the differences between us, and to help people in need whenever I can."

- "I will do everthing I can to reduce my own impact on the environment, to protect other creatures, and to celebrate the beauty of the Earth."

If you agree, sign it. Live by it.

Though it's not a passport that allows you to cross international borders, it may make you aware of barriers in your own mind, and inspire you with the idea that thousands of other young people are making the same commitment.

The passport is your physical connection to the ideas we have worked out for the UN of the Future. We don't know exactly how the United Nations will be transformed, but order a Passport to the Future to be a part of it.

Excited? Surprised? Inspired? Take action!

Jana Kemp

Passport to the Future

JUST THINK WHAT WE COULD DO TOGETHER OVER THE NEXT 50 YEARS!

TO RECEIVE YOUR PASSPORT, WRITE TO A UNA OR DIRECTLY TO US IN CARE OF:
Rescue Mission Headquarters
The White House
Buntingford, England SG9 9AH

History *of the* Future

YUN Daily News 2001–2045

May 1, 2015
Abuse of children's rights stop when Blue Jeans work in cooperation with UNICEF to set up peer-to-peer monitoring.

July 27, 2013
Youth WHO (Yoo-who!) created to promote preventive health care.

April 11, 2018
Universal Peace Pact signed! Nations surrender control of weapons of mass destruction to UN committee. Pact is signed in a very enthusiastic atmosphere: there were no victors and more importantly, no vanquished.

August 14, 2022
Youth Branch of International Court of Justice set up as court of appeal for individual citizens.

June 26, 2045
UN Secretary-General celebrates the centennial of the signing of the UN Charter with the publication of a new children's history of the United Nations that declares "Poverty is over!" No person on earth goes to bed hungry—and every child has a bed to go to!

October 18, 2035
Unlimited free energy available to the developing world as a result of the discovery of super-charged solar cells and the super-conservation programs instituted by Youth Research Programs.

May 22, 2033
Blue Jeans celebrate the graduation of their billionth service volunteer. The UN Youth Service is now the most popular global service group in the world. Everyone wants to join!

Above: *Vajda Vatucte, 19, Lithuania*

84

November 22, 2001

UN General Assembly Resolution sets up Youth Codirector for Youth Unit.

July 31, 2011

Youth Unit Education programs teach everyone to read in 18 months! Young people all over the world know that creating a youth-run Youth Unit was a great idea.

May 10, 2006

UN Youth Service, the Blue Jeans, brings peace to several warring nations with rock concerts and youth-for-peace programs, ignoring soldiers requests to leave them alone to fight in peace.

November 26, 2023

Home for last refugee found by UNHCR. Refugee camps now used as camping and recreation centers.

December 31, 2024

UN TV is the most popular global TV channel this year. UN youth programs head the ratings and bag three Emmys!

May 6, 2025

Governments agree to UN laws against corruption. Leaders can be jailed for stealing public money. Powerful lobbying by UN Youth Unit.

July 27, 2027

Hardwood substitute developed from seaweed. Rain forests increase in size for the first time in a century.

January 1, 2030

Population under control through completion of sex education program.

UNiverse of the Future

Welcome to the UNiverse of the Future. This is your automated attendant. If you would like a tour, please maintain this signal connection and transfer all control of the space vehicle from which you are calling to the attendant.

Waiting.

Connecting.

Initiating.

Welcome to the guided tour. Please do not look directly at the sun without engaging the solar shield. There are two exit doors located at two points on the shuttle. In the event of an on-land emergency landing, please slide down the safety chutes. If an in-space full stop is necessary, your seat cushion may be used as a flotation device.

·On your left, you see Earth. It has no more pollution. The ozone has been restored, and all environmental problems have been solved.

On your right, just above that asteroid, is Mars. A colony was set up there in 2024. The United Nations funded the exploration and every nation on Earth was involved.

Please notice straight ahead, Planet UN, home of the United Nations. It was created by an Instaplanet brand Just-Add-Water Planet Kit. Planet UN has acquired over thirty moons. Each division of the United Nations has its own moon. On the viewscreen, you can see the moons UNESCO and UNICEF. UNICEF was in a solar eclipse just two hours ago.

Passing us on the left is Mercury. While the universe relies on Mercury as a source of Mushroomititus seedfruit snacks, it also provides spectacular views of transits in front of the sun between Venus and Earth.

The guided tour is now over. Please feel free to rocket around at your leisure. Neptunian translators are avaliable at the information asteroid. Thank you for using the guided tour. Your credit card has been charged for two World Dollars. Remember, Spaceport has duty-free shopping!

Disconnecting.

Left: *Cecilia Weckström, 19, Finland*

Next Pages: *Nattapon Limsirikiat, no age given, Thailand*

August 14, 2045

Consumer Relations Department
World Manufacturing Ltd.

Dear Sir/Madam,

      With regard to your recent catalog which
describes your supplies for the next decade:
      I am sure that there will not be much need
for the exhaust fumes and chemical-filled water you
advertise on page nine. They are a bit cheaper than
the clean air and water appearing on later pages,
but much more unpleasant.
      The wars you offer on pages 15-18 seem
terribly unnecessary. I had hoped that you would
not be repeating these offers from your last
catalog. However, I was not at all attracted by
your two-for-the-price-of-one oil slick-and-war
special bargain, and the family-sized World War is
appalling. I intend to order your alternative peace
contracts and help-the-refugees offers, even though
the prices have not been lowered.
      I see you have devoted thirty pages to
crime, even some new varieties. I should
congratulate your staff, but I don't think this
sort of temptation is fair.
      Your marketing campaign needs a little
work, but I shall send in my order in a few days.

Yours faithfully,
A Consumer

                              —*Imogen Goodyear, 15, United Kingdom*

THE GARDEN WE PLANTED TOGETHER

From all over the world
together they came,
to make a garden
with shovels and spades.

Disagreement crept in—
which flowers to grow?
So they sat in a circle
and agreed row by row.

They wrote down their rules
in a big, mighty book
and promised to keep them
by hook and by crook.

With the book to guide them,
they grew beautiful flowers,
each of them equal,
none higher, none lower.

When some flowers grow weak
or ready to die,
the children get together,
new solutions to try.

They share water and seeds,
all must have enough,
the book just demands it
when the going gets tough.

The garden remains a symbol to all,
its flowers are fifty years old this fall.
The book is known as a charter of
*   peace—*
its rules are still valid, so read if you
*   please.*

—Anuruddha Bose, 11, India

Right: *Jittikarn Jariyastien, 11, Thailand*

90

Acknowledgments

This book would not have been possible without the work of thousands of young people from all around the world. For several months, our headquarters was swamped with hundreds of paintings, poems, reports, and stories on the UN. Choosing from them was very hard! To all of you who sent us your creative work, we are immensely grateful for your wonderful contributions and your help. We would have liked to include many more excellent pieces, but we couldn't fit them all in. We have made every effort to credit all contributors correctly. Please let us know if we have made any omissions or errors.

Algeria
Many schools via Algerian Embassy, London, UK
Argentina
St. Catherine's School-Buenos Aires
FUNDECMA, San Miguel de Tucumán
Rolando Robles, San Miguel de Tucumán
Escuela Nacional Superior de Comercio Nº2, Rosario
Asociación Para el Progreso de la Educación, Soledad Vogliano, Córdoba
Australia
UN Youth Association members and friends across Australia
Austria
Salzburg International Preparatory School
Renate Trimmel
Bangladesh
Government Laboratory High School
UNICEF, Dhaka
Belarus
UNESCO Club, Minsk
Peace Child Club, Gomel
Belgium
Koninklijk Lyceum, Antwerp
St John's International School, Waterloo
École Polytechnique de Seraing
Antwerp Middleschool 2
Brazil
Escola Technica da UFPR, Curitiba
Asociaçao Super-Eco, Sao Paolo
Rodrigo Cancellier
Bulgaria
English Language School, Rousse
Svetlana Todorova Kineva
School for European Languages
Svetla Krasimirova Angelova
Cameroon
Joseph Ndjami
Canada
United Nations Club, Ontario
Rescue Mission group, Ontario
Chad
Ecole EHP Les Sounds
Lycee F Eboue, Nidjamena
Chile
German School, Santiago
Liceo Jovina Naranjo, Arica
China
Several contributors through State Education Commission and friends across China
Colombia
Raúl Fernandez Buelvas
Ma. Carolina Vergara
Mario E. Ramirez Rojas

José F. P. Torres
Leila Kalach
Croatia
Peace Child Group "Krug," Zagreb
Croatian Club for the UN
Primary School, Osijek
Cyprus
English School UN Group, Nicosia
American Academy, Larnaca
Czech Republic
32 Basic School, Plzen
Eco-UNESCO Club, Olomouc
Denmark
Kavita Harwani, Copenhagen
Lise Jensen
Ecuador
Alicia Hidalgo
Egypt
American International School, Cairo
Eritrea
Secondary Schools in Asmara, Hamasien and Seraye provinces
Ethiopia
Social Science School
Chercher School, Asepe Tekeri
Finland
Boställsskolan, Esbo
Hagelstamska högstadiet
Helsingin Kuvataidelukio
Helsingin Saksalainen koulu
International School of Helsinki
Katedralsskolan, Åbo
Kimito gymnasium
Kivistön koulu
Kurkelan ala-aste
Kymenkartanon lukio, Heinola
Laajalahden Koulu, Espoo
Langinkosken Lukio, Kotka
Länsi-Puijon ala-aste
Mattlidens gymnasium, Esbo
Oulun normaalikoulu
Pilvi Keränen, Turku
Paloheinän ala-aste, Helsinki
Puijonsarven Ya, Kuopio
Puistolan yläaste, Helsinki
Puolalanmäki Upper Secondary School, Turku
Roihuvuoren ala-aste
Tönnön koulu, Orimattila
France
European Business Programme, France
Groupe ESC, Bordeaux
Jules Verne Ecole & Club UNESCO, Chamiers
Beatrice Tanaka
Club UNESCO-ECG de Blitta-Gare
Associated Schools Programme UNESCO, Paris

Gambia
Kerr Ardo Primary School
Germany
Ulrike Heitmeier, UPS Viersen
Ghana
UN Students and Youth Association
Greece
Tasis Hellenic International School, Athens
Lakoniki School, Athens
Hungary
American International School, Budapest
India
Peace Child Group, New Delhi
Bhavan's Mehta Vidyashram, Allahabad
O.P. Tripathi
Gaurav Agarwal
Manava Bharati International School,
New Delhi
Soma Chakraborty
Tamilnadu United Nations Assocation,
Madras
Government High School Pati,
Pithouragarh
St. Xavier's School, West Bengal
The Alpha Movement, Calcutta
Birla Vidya Niketan, Pilani
Sonia Kukreja, New Delhi
Vidya Vikasini Mat. Hr. Secondary School,
Coimbatore
Indonesia
Rama International School, Purwakarta
Iran
Ferdowsi, Tehran
Italy
Viola Caretti
Scuola Media "F Torracai," Matera
Scuola Media Statale, Varazze
Liceo Classico, La Spezia
Japan
Peace Child Hiroshima
Kazakhstan
School No. 59
Kenya
Shieywe Secondary School, Kakamega
J. Omaya
Precious Blood Secondary School, Riruta
Complexe Scolaire Salisa
Lenana School
Kuwait
Lakshmi Simhan
American School of Kuwait, Hawalli
Lithuania
Kaunas Secondary School
Daukantas Secondary School, Papile
Lina Salanauskaite
National Commission for UNESCO,
Vilnius
Kauno Verzvu Secondary School, Kaunas
Madagascar
Lycee Laurent Botokeky, Tulear
Bakolimirima Robertnie
Malta
Girl's Secondary School, Mosta
Lily of the Valley School
Mexico
Many Schools via Mexican Embassy,
United Kingdom
Colegio Morelos de Cuernavaca
Mongolia
Mongolian-Russian School N°3, Aygul
Morocco
Ecole Al Fadica, Zemamra

Netherlands
Deutshe Schule, The Hague
Joram Grünfeld
American International School, Rotterdam
New Zealand
Nga Tawa School
Nigeria
Tumaculate Conception School, Ugo
Bayero University, Kano
Norway
Utøy Skauen Ungdomsskor
Philippines
Rajou Soliman High School UNESCO
Club
Children and Peace, Jasus Quezon City
Philippines Women's University, Manila
P Urduja Elementary School, Manila
Badian National High School, Cebu
Poland
Defending Rights & Dignity of Children,
Chorzow
Ozone Group, Vi Liceum, Krakow
Liceum Ogølnoksztalcace, Torum
II LO Im J.S. Deckiego
Justyna Lesko
Tespoi School Ogolmokent, Poolloslie
Szkola Podstawowa 113, Wroclaw
Portugal
Escola Secundaria D. de Duarte, Coimbra
Instituto Politécnico Du Porto
Russia
Peace Child Group, Tver Region
English Grammar School N° 1509,
Moscow
Physico-Technical Lyceum W1, Saratov
English Secondary School 1016, Moscow
UNESCO Foundation
Marina Svagina
Peace Child, Krasnoyarsk
Senegal
EFI UNESCO School, Thies
Sierra Leone
Peace Child, Sierra Leone
Port Loko UN Student Association
Singapore
Bahai Youth Committee
Slovakia
Gymnazium, Poprad
Gymnázium Hubeného 23, Bratislava
Gymnazium, Tajovskemo
Slovenija
Osnova Sola Ciril Kosmac, Piran
Srednja Sola, Slovenj Gradec
South Africa
Rondebosch Boys High School
Somalia
Merrick Fall
Spain
Manuel Antonio Fernandez
J.A.Fernandez Perez
The American Community College of
Asturias
Marta Abella Pérez
Escola Pública Marinada
Salvador Espriu, Barcelona
IFP A Pinquela
Colegio Público "Gloria Fuertes,"
Andorra
Colegio "Carmelitas"
APAS, Madrid
Sweden
Sigtuna School

Switzerland
International School, Geneva
Tanzania
Amani UNESCO Club, Mtwara
Roots & Shoots, Zanzibar
Thailand
International School Bangkok
Trinidad
Asja Girls UNESCO
Turkey
Many schools via Turkish Embassy,
London, UK
U. Savas Baran Yazanblars
Skaun Ungdom Skole
Ukraine
Tatiana Urodova
Secondary School N°2, Odessa
United Kingdom
Lomond School
Honorable Cultural Attache to the
Armenian Embassy
Newport Free Grammar School
Lliswerry High School, Newport
Bishopshalt School, Hillington
St. Edmund's College, Herts
Poyton County High School, Cheshire
Millais School, West Sussex
O. Gillman, West Sussex
Daniel P. Moynihan, West Hartford
One World Trust, London
The King's School Cheshire
Hamble School, Hants
YSGOL Pencoed School
Great Hormead School
St. Mary's School, Bisop's Stortford
United States of America
Many schools via Paintbrush Diplomacy,
San Francisco
Klub Tribe, Los Angeles
Travis High School, Austin
The Robert Muller School, Austin
United Nations Association: Children as
Peacemakers
AARP (Janet Koster)
Caleb Green Wood School
United Nations International School,
New York
Uruguay
Escuela N°1, Tacuarembó
Yugoslavia
Peace Child Kosova
Ivan Sekulovic, Belgrade
Peacock Club, Xharra
Zaire
Lycee Motema MPIKO, Kinshasa
Complexe Scolaire Diema
Club et Ecole Associee, UNESCO,
Kinshasa
Complexe Scolaire 12 Septembre,
Kinshasa
E. P. M. Bokeleale
Zambia
Life Link, Ndola
National Commission for UNESCO,
Lusaka

We would like to thank the UNESCO Associated Schools project from which many of these contributors came. We would also like to give special thanks to David and Rosey for their great support and patience; and to Natasha and Alexander for sharing their home with us. You're great!

Index

Just some of the people who put this book together for you!

Photograph taken by: *David Woollcombe*

WHAT THE WORLD NEEDS

A little more kindnesss, a little less need,
A little more giving, a little less greed,
A little more gladness, a little less care,
A little more faith, a little more prayer,
A little more "we" and a little less "I,"
A little more laughter and a little less sigh,
A little more sunshine brightening the view,
And a lot more friends, exactly like you.
    —Elzbieta Jaworska, 15, Poland

Left: *Cecilia Weckström, 19, Finland*